THE V

*Also available from Headline Liaison*

Seven Days by J J Duke
Dangerous Desires by J J Duke
The Journal by James Allen
Love Letters by James Allen
Aphrodisia by Rebecca Ambrose
Out of Control by Rebecca Ambrose
A Private Affair by Carol Anderson
Voluptuous Voyage by Lacey Carlyle
Magnolia Moon by Lacey Carlyle
The Paradise Garden by Aurelia Clifford
The Golden Cage by Aurelia Clifford
Vermilion Gates by Lucinda Chester
Sleepless Nights by Tom Crewe & Amber Wells
Hearts on Fire by Tom Crewe and Amber Wells
A Scent of Danger by Sarah Hope-Walker

# The Ways of a Woman

J J Duke

Copyright © J J Duke 1997

The right of J J Duke to be identified as the Author
of the Work has been asserted by him in accordance with
the Copyright, Designs and Patents Act 1988.

First published in 1997
by HEADLINE BOOK PUBLISHING

A HEADLINE LIAISON paperback

10 9 8 7 6 5 4 3 2 1

All rights reserved. No part of this publication may be
reproduced, stored in a retrieval system, or transmitted,
in any form or by any means without the prior written
permission of the publisher, nor be otherwise circulated
in any form of binding or cover other than that in which
it is published and without a similar condition being
imposed on the subsequent purchaser.

All characters in this publication are fictitious
and any resemblance to real persons, living or dead,
is purely coincidental.

Similarly, all businesses described in this book are fictitious
and any resemblance to companies that may exist now,
or in the future, is entirely coincidental.

ISBN 0 7472 5443 5

Typeset by CBS, Felixstowe, Suffolk

Printed and bound in Great Britain by
Cox & Wyman Ltd, Reading, Berks

HEADLINE BOOK PUBLISHING
A division of Hodder Headline PLC
338 Euston Road
London NW1 3BH

# The Ways of a Woman

# Chapter One

'We shouldn't be doing this.'

'Why not?'

'You're married.'

'I told you, I'm getting a divorce.'

He kissed her again, sliding his tongue into her mouth and twisting it around. He was a good kisser. He sucked at her lips while his hands caressed her back. Paula could feel his erection hardening against her belly.

It felt a little like being a teenager again, smooching on the front porch outside her parent's house, hoping they wouldn't come out. But this was her house and there was no one inside.

She pulled away from him and took her keys from her handbag. Opening the front door she led him into the hall trying to forget her misgivings. It had been at least six months since she'd been to bed with a man. She thought she should feel a sense of excitement, of arousal even. But the only thing she felt was apprehension. Paula knew what she wanted from a man, she knew what would arouse her. But she had the feeling that Simon Leonard, standing awkwardly in her hall, shifting his weight from one foot to the other and looking distinctly uncomfortable, was not going to give it to her.

'Nice,' he said with little enthusiasm, looking around. The hall was decorated in an eau-de-nil wallpaper with tiny blue flowers.

'Thanks. Do you want a drink?'

'I think I've had enough already.'

'What, then?' she said wanting him to take the initiative.

Tonight had been the twentieth anniversary of the company she worked for. They'd celebrated with a party at Claridges and invited at least a hundred people from all the firms they did business with. Stockbrokers and merchant bankers in their Savile Row suits drank champagne cocktails and ate chicken vol-au-vents while their wives, in over-formal dresses with boned bodices had chatted to each other about their country gardens, horses and dogs. Simon Leonard had made a beeline for her and spent all evening trying to talk her into bed. Against her better judgment she'd finally succumbed to his somewhat elusive charm. Now, curiously, having won the prize he didn't seem so keen.

The sitting room door was open and he wandered through it, looking around. He studied her collection of books displayed in two racks of shelving on either side of the breast of the fireplace. He moved to the pictures on the white-painted walls. It was obvious he was not going to be the one to say the magic words.

'Shall I show you the bedroom?' Paula couldn't keep a note of irritation out of her voice.

'Mmm . . . sounds interesting,' he said, grinning. 'You're really great looking, you know.'

'So you said.' She wasn't unattractive, she knew that. She had large green eyes, and a small straight nose, with a mouth that was perfectly symmetrical. Her lips were very smooth and slightly pouted, and her cheekbones were round and high.

'Lead on,' he prompted.

She walked upstairs. He followed her. Paula was intensely aware of his eyes on her buttocks, tightly covered by the silk of her one-and-only salmon-pink cocktail dress. She suspected he was hanging back, trying to see more of her long legs sheathed in sheer black nylon.

'Nice legs,' he muttered.

She pretended not to hear. The house was a small Victorian terrace in Fulham, a two-up, two-down with a back addition. The bedroom had just enough room for a double bed, a single bedside table, a small pine wardrobe and a chest of drawers. With the money from her divorce settlement she had managed to afford a few alterations. The kitchen had been extended at the back of the house, and she'd had another bathroom built on top of it, connecting directly to her bedroom.

'Make yourself at home,' she said heading for the bathroom. She closed the door behind her and tried not to panic. What on earth did she think she was doing? He wasn't even a stunning hunk. Simon Leonard was rather chubby with a button nose and small, round eyes. It had been his persistence that had attracted her. It was a long time since a man had made such a conscious effort to flatter and cajole her into bed. It wasn't that she was plain, at least she didn't think so. But she knew she gave off negative waves that discouraged most men more effectively than an ugly face.

Paula tried to push aside her doubts. She'd wanted to get laid, hadn't she? Wasn't that what this was all about, to put it crudely? He was a good kisser. Hopefully he'd be a good lover too.

Quickly she unzipped her dress and pulled it off. She was wearing a white cotton bra that had been washed too many times and was now almost grey, and navy-blue cotton knickers. Hardly seductive. She hadn't dressed with this sort of end to the evening in mind. Reaching behind her back she unclipped her bra. She pulled her knickers off with her tights. If she had had the courage she would have liked to bound back into the room naked, throw herself on the bed and cry out for him to take her. But she didn't. Not that her body wasn't good enough. She exercised regularly and watched her weight and she had a trim, slim figure with a narrow waist, a flat belly, and pert, round buttocks. Her legs were long and slender and her breasts, which she had always thought of as her best feature were full and spherical, supporting their own weight without sagging so they were high on her chest.

Wishing she was made of stronger stuff, she slipped into her pink towelling robe, knotted its belt around her and combed her dark brown, wavy hair in the mirror. Her dark green eyes stared back at her, reflecting a sort of forlorn hope. She took a metaphorical deep breath as she opened the bathroom door.

All Simon Leonard's clothes were hanging from the brass hook at the back of the bedroom door and he was lying naked under her blue-and-yellow patterned duvet, staring up at the ceiling with his hands laced behind his head. He'd turned off the overhead light and turned on the small bedside lamp.

'Hi,' he said, grinning.

'Hi,' she answered, for want of something better to say. She sat on the edge of the bed.

'You're gorgeous,' he said. 'I really think you're gorgeous. You don't make the best of yourself, you know.' He sat up and put his hand over hers. The duvet fell away from his chest. He had a thick layer of fat covering his ribs and his flesh was white. There were three or four very long black hairs around each nipple but apart from these his chest was hairless.

His hand moved to her cheek and she twisted round to kiss him again. As his tongue pushed into her mouth his hand slid down the front of her robe, parting the folds of material and slipping inside to cup her right breast. He squeezed it hard then rolled her nipple between his fingers. His hand dropped down to the belt of the robe, and unknotted it. Moving up again, it pushed the robe off her shoulders and down to her waist as his mouth moved on to her neck. He kissed and licked and sucked at her flesh, working his way down over her shoulders and collar-bone until he got to her breasts. As his mouth centred itself on her right nipple he pushed her back on the bed.

Paula felt both nipples stiffen at this assault. His mouth closed around the puckered flesh, pushing it back with his tongue, then tweaking it between his teeth. This was a lot better she thought. A sense of excitement – finally – began to make her pulse race. As his hand delved into her lap she parted her legs. Her brown pubic hair looked as though it had been cropped but it grew like that naturally. Each hair was short, and each pointed inward and downward to the apex of her thighs. His hand took the same direction. He inserted a single finger into the crease of her labia.

'You've got a wonderful body,' he said, the compliments coming in an endless succession.

Paula didn't reply. Instead she fished under the duvet. Her hand encountered a round belly at the base of which his cock was standing up almost vertically. She wrapped her fingers around it. She had never really known what to do with this appendage. She was not very practised in the art of sexual encounters. Awkwardly she squeezed it, then slid the ring of her fingers down the whole shaft and up again. His finger, meanwhile, was wriggling down to her vagina. Finding the entrance he pushed up into her. She was a little surprised to discover that her sex was wet. The lubrication made it easy for him to thrust his finger higher.

His legs were under the duvet while she was on top of it.

She tried to pull the bedding back but her own body stopped her. Simon tried too, but the only way to disentangle themselves from the duvet was to stop what they were doing. Instead, Simon tried to roll over on to the other half of the bed and pull her under the duvet with him, but this only made matters worse. Her body was crushed against his but the duvet was still between them.

'Wait,' she said, accepting the fact they would have to part. She let go of his erection and struggled to sit up, hauling the bedding off both of them and throwing her towelling robe on to the floor. 'That's better,' she said trying not to look at his naked body. She didn't want to be disappointed.

Simon caught her hand and pulled her towards him. He wrapped both arms around her and rolled on top of her, thrusting his thighs between her legs and forcing them open. She wanted more foreplay. She wanted to be kissed and caressed and aroused but he had other ideas. He bucked his hips and she felt his cock prod against her clitoris then immediately slide down the well lubricated furrow of her labia, to her vagina. He wriggled forward and it plunged into her.

'Lovely,' he said, his face buried in her neck, his voice dropping an octave. 'You're so lovely, so beautiful.' It was as though the repetitive compliments were part of his sexual technique.

In this position the penetration was shallow but he did not try to push any deeper. Instead, he just squirmed around inside her almost imperceptibly. Yet again, Paula took the initiative. She raised her legs in the air and pulled her thighs back towards her body so her sex was tilted up towards him and his cock couldn't help but be propelled into her more fully.

This appeared to galvanise him into action. He began to move in and out of her. He moved quickly with small, jerky movements, his face remaining firmly buried against her neck. He made odd grunting noises with every inward thrust.

Neither the new position nor the pumping action improved what Paula felt. She had no sense of being possessed, of being filled, no overwhelming flood of passion.

Relentless, like a mechanical toy that had been wound up and would run on until its spring gave out, he continued thrusting. Paula closed her eyes. She imagined a giant clockwork key, turning in the middle of his back. She began to think about the party, and the conversation she'd had with Aaron Lichtman, chairman and chief executive of Lichtman Terry Associates, her employers. He had been complimentary about her work and told her she was a valued employee.

Suddenly, Simon's body went rigid. He made a noise that sounded like a strangulated cough. She didn't feel his cock jerk or kick inside her, but became aware of a flood of liquid heat running along the walls of her vagina. In seconds his body went limp and he rolled off her.

'Lovely,' he said without looking at her. 'Great,' he elaborated.

She looked down at his body. His erection was glistening wet and withering rapidly. She glanced up at his face, but he was not looking at her. He appeared to be searching for something on the bedroom floor.

'What's the matter?' she asked.

'Can't find my socks,' he said.

As far as he was concerned the evening was obviously over.

Paula stepped out of the bath and wrapped her body in a large pink bath towel. As she walked through into the bedroom, plugged in her hairdryer and began drying her hair, she thought about last night.

She had always known what she wanted from a man. At least she thought she did. She wanted to be ravished. She remembered first reading that word in some tacky teenage girl's magazine. She'd looked it up. It was from the French *ravir*, to enrapture, and the Latin, *rapere*, to seize and carry off. That's exactly what she wanted from a man, and exactly what she had never had, to date. There was a distinction between ravishment and rape, of course. She had never had fantasies about being raped, but she dreamt about being seized and enraptured.

What that meant for her, the scenarios that fleshed out the skeleton of the fantasy, might be different in detail, but in essence was always the same. She was always fully clothed. Not naked or dressed in a flimsy chiffon negligee with no panties, but wearing a dress or a suit and a full complement of underwear. Tights even. That was the point as far as she was concerned. The need, his need – the imaginary, mythical man-of-her-dream's needs – had to be so urgent, so compelling that he could not wait for her to calmly take off her clothes. They would have to be torn off, ripped away. He would have to carry her away too. That was another requirement. He would need to sweep her into his arms, kiss her hard on the mouth and carry her to his bed. The rest was hazy. How and what he would do to her she could not imagine, never having experienced such passion. She only knew that at the end of it she would be a whimpering heap, unable to do anything but beg for mercy, beg for him to stop, which, naturally, he would not do.

Not that the assorted variations she worked out along these lines were anything more than pleasant, rather abstract daydreams. She supposed that was what gave her a tingle of sexual excitement. But it was never more than that. They were not dreams she conjured up as a prelude to masturbation.

Not at all. She had always found masturbation a chore, at best a momentary diversion, at worst a total void, serving to remind her of how unsatisfying this aspect of her life had always been. At one time she had conscientiously attempted it on a regular basis, more in hope than passion, but now it was something in which she rarely indulged.

But that didn't mean she could go through life without sex rearing its ugly head. In recent weeks she had become more and more conscious of her lack of experience in this area. It bothered her though she had no idea why, out of the blue, it should. It never had before. After a few minor and desultory sexual experiences at university, her main sexual adventures had been with the man she'd subsequently married and recently divorced, and he could never have been described as exciting. She had always told herself that she must have a very low sex drive. Andy, her ex, had occasionally given her an orgasm, but that was hardly a cause for major celebrations. The earth had never moved. In fact, it had barely trembled.

Paula had always thought his sex drive was low too, and that this made them compatible. After the first couple of months of enthusiasm for her body, his need for her had been strictly limited and highly regular, every second Tuesday to be precise.

It suited her. Paula had her career and that was more important to her than anything else. Paula was a woman who liked to succeed and her career was blossoming. She was the youngest ever senior executive Lichtman Terry had ever appointed. Striving for sexual pleasure on the other hand reminded her only of failure. Every second Tuesday she had done her best to please her husband and, as he appeared perfectly satisfied with the arrangement, she imagined it suited him too.

It didn't. She had been sent to a conference in Amsterdam

on the integration of European gilt markets, taking an evening flight to be ready for an early start the following morning. At the airport she'd been told that all the ground crews had walked out in a dispute over handling levels. No flights would leave Heathrow that night. She'd taken a taxi home. When she'd called out to her husband as she'd walked in through the door, there had been no reply and though the lights were still on she'd assumed he'd gone out to the pub. Walking upstairs to take a bath, she'd gone straight to their bedroom. There she had discovered the real reason Andy had not replied. He couldn't. His mouth was full, stuffed with a pair of black lacy panties which were held in place by a black stocking tied around his head. He was in no position to be able to pull them out either. He was spread-eagled across their double bed, attached to each corner of the antique brass bedstead by metal handcuffs. A slender blonde had been desperately trying to get the key into one of the small locks that secured the cuffs in place as Paula walked into the room. The blonde was wearing black, patent leather thigh boots with a six-inch heel and nothing else. Despite her slim figure she had the biggest bosom Paula had ever seen. Her breasts hung down to her waist.

That had been a year ago. The divorce had been relatively painless. Walking into the bedroom at that moment had crystallised two things for Paula. The first was that she had never really known her husband at all, and the second was that she didn't care that she hadn't. She didn't care for him at all. They had divided up their assets and Paula had kept the double bed and the brass bedstead as a sort of *memento mori*.

Finding that Andy's attitude to sex was not as advertised had not, however, changed her own. She had absolutely no desire to be cuffed to a brass bedstead, or, on the other hand, wield the whip that she had subsequently discovered was part of the service her husband had paid the big-breasted prostitute for. Nor had Paula gone on a sexual rampage, as some of her friends had done when their marriages had ended as a result of a husband's infidelity. In fact, her experience had made her interest in sex decline further. Her career, she decided, was all the excitement she needed.

Now, despite this resolution, something was stirring in her libido. She had only had one man since the divorce. She had gone to bed with Simon Leonard, primarily, she supposed, to prove to herself once again that sexual relationships with men were just not something she was good at. It had also proved to her that she seemed to attract – and be attracted to – men whose idea of sexual ecstasy was about as interesting as watching paint dry. Not that she could cast the first stone in that department. Her sexuality was hardly incandescent. The truth was, she told herself, that last night had proved that sex was very low on her agenda. Nothing had changed. Hopefully her body would resume its famed indifference on the subject for at least another six months.

She finished drying her hair. Stripping off the bath towel, she began pulling on her work clothes; a functional cotton bra and knickers and a beige shirt-waister dress. She wore heavy, knitted dark-brown tights and suede boots. It was cold outside. Perfunctorily, she dusted her eyes with eye-shadow and applied a light pink lipstick, more to protect her lips from chapping in the cold air than for any cosmetic reason. She brushed her dark-brown, wavy hair and went downstairs, collecting her heavy coat from the coat stand by the front door.

It was eight-fifteen. Despite the exertions of last night she had got up early, determined to keep to her plan of doing the weekend shopping at the local supermarket before she went to work. At eight twenty-eight she was pulling into the car park and by nine was transferring two boxes of the provisions into the boot of her small, but relatively new and well-accessorised, Rover. Just as she was about to close the boot a sleek, dark blue Mercedes 450SL drew into the space next to hers. She caught sight of its driver's shock of long blonde hair but not the driver's face.

'Paula!' a voice called out loudly as she unlocked the car door to get behind the wheel. She looked round. The blonde was standing by the open door of the Mercedes her mouth gaping open in surprise.

'It is you, isn't it? Paula, don't you recognise me?'

Like a television picture coming into focus, the minor changes six years had wrought on the woman's face resolved into an image that Paula recognised and she found herself staring into a face she had known, at one time, almost better than her own. Catherine Bidmead had been her best friend at university. They had shared a room in college and subsequently set up a flat together in London for two years.

'Catherine. My God, Catherine!'

They stood staring, both totally transfixed for a moment, the coincidence of meeting like this stunning them both. Then they ran into each other's arms hugging and patting each other on the back, as is customary with long lost friends.

'Let me look at you,' Paula said pulling Catherine back and holding her at arm's length. 'You look wonderful.'

It was true. Catherine was gorgeous. But then she always had been. Her long blonde hair cascaded down over her shoulders like a waterfall of liquid gold, glinting in the light. Her face had strong bold features with big blue eyes that sparkled with life, a long straight nose and high cheekbones. She had a large, fleshy mouth and her lips were naturally a deep ruby red. She bore her head proudly on a long slender neck which added to the impression of height. Her figure was curvaceous, her breasts jutting out firmly, her waist cinched and her hips generous. She wore tight, brown leather trousers and a cream silk blouse through which a white lacy bra could be seen as the front of her wolf skin fur coat was unbuttoned.

'I wish I could say the same for you,' she said to Paula sharply. They had never minced words with each other. Their relationship had always been based on mutual respect for each other which made honesty easy and inoffensive.

'I know. I'm on my way to work.'

'Haven't you ever heard of power-dressing?'

They laughed.

'It's good to see you. When did you get back?' Paula asked.

'Two months. No, less. Five weeks. I tried your number. Disconnected.'

'Didn't you get my letter?'

'No.'

'I wrote when I moved. I wondered why I hadn't heard from you. I thought you must be busy.'

'I guess it crossed the Atlantic the same time I did but in the opposite direction. It's just as well we bumped into each other. What are you doing tonight?'

'Nothing.' That was an easy question to answer.

'Come round to dinner then. I'll go and get something special.' Catherine nodded towards the supermarket.

'Great.' Paula looked at her watch. 'Look I've got to run. I've got a meeting at nine-thirty and I can't be late for it.'

'Here . . .' Catherine delved into her Hermes bag and pulled out a little tortoiseshell card case. She opened it and handed Paula a white card. 'Here's the address. We can talk all night. About eight?'

'Wonderful. It's good to see you again.'
And it was.

The address on the card was, like the supermarket where they'd met, five minutes from Paula's house. It was on the borders of Fulham and Chelsea in a wide, tree-lined avenue, with detached houses from the early Victorian period, all of different designs and all further distinguished by various later additions including, most recently, large garages and driveways.

Catherine Bidmead and Paula Lindsey had been unlikely friends. Paula had been bookish, intense and academically ambitious; Catherine was lazy, relaxed and apparently without a care in the world. While Paula would spend her last penny on a new edition of medieval Mystery plays, Catherine would have gone for a lacy black teddy to impress a boyfriend – or, more often boyfriends, as they were never singular. Paula found men's company a limited compensation for not studying. Catherine, on the other hand, appeared to find men totally fascinating and an endless excuse not to pick up a book or write an essay.

But this diversity created a bond between them. They had sat up night after night, talking and laughing and putting the world to rights. Paula could never understand why Catherine took the world so lightly; Catherine could never understand why Paula treated everything with such seriousness. They debated for hours, each determined to show the other a better way, though both knew, in the end, neither would ever change.

Predictably Paula had got a first. Catherine had surprised her friend by scraping a third. They had moved to London together and while Paula got a job in a stockbroker's graduate training scheme, Catherine got by on the largesse of men, who were only too happy, it appeared, to give generous donations to the cause of keeping her in relative luxury in return for being seen in her company and being allowed in her bed. After two years of flitting from one man to the next, Catherine had met Max Von Reichbach from New York. She had married him two months later and left on Concorde promising to write to Paula every week. After a couple of years the letters had dried up. She would call occasionally and send Christmas cards, but that was all. Paula soon stopped writing too, but had written to her after the divorce to send her the change of address and new telephone number. Their relationship, Paula told herself, had been a victim of geography, impossible to keep up in the face of such physical distance.

Now, as Paula parked her car in Catherine's driveway, it was perfectly clear to her that their friendship was not dead or dying, but merely put on hold until circumstances permitted it to be resumed. From their brief encounter in the supermarket car park she was confident they would pick up from exactly where they had left off six years before.

Paula had gone out in her lunch hour and bought a bottle of Dom Perignon and a bunch of white lilies because they had always been Catherine's favourite flowers. She walked up to the front door with the two gifts in her arms.

'Hi!' The door was flung open before she could ring the bell. Catherine was wearing a blouson-style cream silk top and matching trousers so full and loose it was difficult to see the dividing line between each leg. Her long hair had been scraped back into a French pleat.

'For you,' Paula said proffering the champagne and flowers.

'You remembered lilies. And Dom Perignon. You must be doing well. Come in.'

Paula stepped across the threshold.

'Obviously not as well as you,' she said looking around. The house was large and lavish. The hall floor was of highly polished rosewood, the walls lined in cream silk. There were two Norwich School watercolours on the wall to the left and a large, brightly coloured oil opposite. It looked as though it might be a Kandinsky.

Catherine led the way into the sitting room which was of the same order of splendour, a huge room stretching the whole length of the house with windows overlooking the front drive and a small, neat garden at the back. There was a large modern kitchen to one side and a conservatory had been constructed at the back of that to serve as a dining room.

There were two large sofas in the rear portion of the room, facing each other and a low, walnut coffee table between them. On the table was a bottle of Louis Roederer Cristal in an eighteenth century silver wine cooler stacked with ice. Next to it were two impossibly thin champagne flutes and a large Baccarrat crystal bowl full of green olives.

'Make yourself at home,' Catherine said flopping into the corner of one of the sofas and pouring the champagne.

'Is this all yours?' Paula said as she sat opposite her friend.

'The spoils of war. That's what my marriage turned out to be. One battle after another.'

'You're divorced?'

'Two months ago. That's why I came home. This place belonged to Max's family. Their London pad. I agreed to take it in exchange for a clean break settlement. No alimony. Pity we didn't live in California I suppose. Then I'd have got much more.'

'Can you afford to run it?'

'With a little help from my friends. Well, one particular friend. Cheers.' She handed Catherine a glass then clinked hers, very delicately against the side of it. They both sipped the chilled wine.

'It's so good to see you. You've hardly changed at all,' Paula said. Being with Catherine made her feel good. It had always been that way.

'So, where do we start? What went wrong with Max? Or do you want to skip that?'

'Sex is what went wrong with Max. Simple as that.'

'You always loved sex.'

'Exactly. And I thought he did too.'

'But he didn't?'

'Oh, he loved sex all right. But not necessarily with me.'

'He was having an affair?'

'We always told each other the truth, didn't we?'

'Always.'

'I've not told anyone else this. After about a year, he told me he'd got this idea. He said he was having fantasies about wanting to watch me with another man. At first, I thought that's all it was. A fantasy. Something he used to think about to get himself turned on. I encouraged it because he always got so hot when he talked about it. I used to talk about it too, pretend he was someone else, all that sort of thing. Then one day he came home and he says he's got this friend in town and can we put him up for the night. We had this big house so it wasn't a problem. The problem was that it was all a set up. He tried to get me really drunk over dinner. Next thing I know, this guy's all over me. Got one hand up my skirt and the other down my blouse and Max is begging me to take my clothes off and give this friend a show. That's how he put it. Give him a show. Well, I agreed. I stripped off. The friend stripped off. Max stripped off. Then we all started romping around and it got complicated. I mean, I'd had a lot to drink and I was losing track of who was doing what to do whom. Whom – is that correct?'

'Yes,' Paula said. 'So what happened?'

'Nothing. Not then. But about a month later Max came home and said he wanted this guy to stay over again. This time it was obvious what was going to happen and, to tell you the truth, I didn't mind at all. You know I've always been into sex. I often used to have two guys in one day, I mean one in the afternoon and a different one in the evening. I did that at uni a couple of times. But I'd never had two at the same time. It was great. Lots of new possibilities. Lots of new feelings. We did very naughty things. You can imagine.'

Paula saw her friend shiver at the memory. 'And?' she prompted.

'It was all the same as before. We had a lot to drink. I stripped off. They stripped off. I started playing with them, doing all sorts of things with them. But then after a while I realised no one was paying much attention to me. There they were doing it together on the carpet, with Max giving this other guy a real hammering. You should have seen the look on his face. I'd never seen him so turned on.'

'He was gay?'

'He'd used me as a way of getting at this guy. Once he'd got him I was surplus to requirements.'

'And you had no idea before that?'

'None. Maybe he changed, who knows?'

'Andy gave me a bit of a surprise too.'

'Really?' Catherine re-filled their champagne glasses.

Paula told her about the big-breasted prostitute and Andy's proclivity for bondage and the whip. Catherine listened open-mouthed.

'I still can't believe we bumped into each other like that,' she said when Paula had finished telling her all the details of her divorce. 'I wasn't sure how I was going to find you again.

I called your old firm when I got back but they wouldn't tell me where you'd gone.'

'They wouldn't. Company policy. In case you were a client and you were going to transfer business to me.'

'So fate was on our side.'

The phone rang. It was perched on a small table at the side of the sofa and Catherine reached over lazily and picked up the receiver. 'Excuse me,' she said to Paula. 'I know who this is. Hello?'

Paula watched her friend's face as she stretched out, putting her feet up on the coffee table and resting her head against the back cushion. She was smiling, a smile Paula remembered well, the smile Catherine always wore when men were around.

'Hello,' she repeated, the tone of her voice lower and deliberately seductive. Paula recognised that too. How many times had see heard her use it to beguile men?

'Black,' Catherine said. 'Lacy black . . . black too, of course . . . You know I never wear tights . . .' Catherine caught Paula's eye and winked. 'Really? Just hearing my voice has done that has it? I don't believe you . . . What are you going to do about it then? I told you I can't make it tonight . . . No . . . No . . . You're being a very bad boy . . . All right, take it out.' Catherine was grinning across at Paula. She made a loop of her thumb and forefinger and pumped it up and down in the air. 'Come on take it out . . . Is that better? I told you, black lace, those tiny little ones with the satin straps . . . Of course nothing else. Just my bra and panties and those black stockings you like so much, the shiny ones . . . No, Doug . . . I'll call you later. Then you can. Make sure you wait . . . Doug, you've just got to wait. Then I might, it depends how I feel . . . Not now . . . Yes, like last time. You haven't forgotten have you? Good. Now be a good boy and go away . . . Bye.'

She dropped the receiver back on to the phone.

'Sorry about that.'

'No need to ask what *he* wanted,' Paula said.

'He wanted a good wank,' Catherine said with the directness that was one of her most enduring traits.

'Is he going to be the next in line?'

'God no, never again. I'm never getting married again Paula. If I ever show any signs of it I give you permission to arrange to have me committed. Come on, let's eat. I'm starving. Talking about sex always makes me hungry.'

'Just like doing it.'

Paula remembered that Catherine would often come home after a heavy date and raid the refrigerator, sitting in the middle of the kitchen floor gorging on whatever she had found.

Catherine had laid the large modern dining table in the middle of the conservatory with solid silver cutlery, delicate porcelain plates, and bell-shaped glasses, together with at least twenty candles in a variety of holders. She served smoked salmon and *boeuf bourguignon* with rice and a large green salad. There were three sorts of cheese and a huge pear and almond tart. Catherine had always been a wonderful cook. It was another difference between them. Where Paula would usually buy pre-cooked food, Catherine would take endless trouble preparing everything freshly herself. It might, of course, have been another reason men found her so irresistible.

But tonight, though the food she had cooked was delicious, it was eaten with barely a comment. The conversation was just too intense. The two women plunged back into each other's lives, their old familiarity making their mutual stories of the last six years a seamless flow of insight and revelation. The wine flowed too, more to lubricate the vocal chords than from any desire to get drunk. But by the time the food was finished and they had consumed most of a bottle of *Beaume de Venise* with the tart, they were both the worse for wear.

'I'm not going to be able to drive home,' Paula said. 'I'll have to get a cab.'

'Don't be silly. You can stay the night. You haven't got to work in the morning.'

'If that's all right?'

'Of course it is. Come on, let's go into the sitting room. Do you want a brandy?'

'If I'm not driving, why not?'

Paula curled up in the corner of one of the sofas while Catherine poured *Hine Antique* into two large balloon glasses and set them down on the coffee table.

'So, who's Doug?'

'He runs an investment bank.'

'Called?'

'Latimer's.'

'You're going out with Doug Latimer!' Paula said with astonishment. Latimer Investment Bank was one of the biggest privately owned banks in the city, having built its reputation on taking big risks, financing companies that other banks had turned down. Latimer's ability to turn potentially huge downside losses into equally huge upside profit had become legendary.

'He's very generous,' Catherine said, smiling broadly.

'Is he married?'

'Separated.'

'And you're his mistress?'

'That's a rather old-fashioned way of looking at it. Actually I'm more like a whore with only one client. I keep him happy sexually and he pays my expenses.'

'That sounds like the ideal arrangement. Is he demanding?'

'Yes. Very. He's good at it too. Got a lovely big cock.'

'Catherine!' Paula said. But her shock was only pantomimed. In the old days Catherine had frequently been just as crude.

'It's true! Mmm . . . I can feel it now.' She stretched out on the sofa, pressing her hand into her lower stomach. 'Right here.'

'You really love sex, don't you?'

'Mmm . . .'

'The trouble is,' Paula said. 'I don't.'

'What makes you say that?'

'Because it's true. I don't enjoy it. I'm not very good at it. I might just as well be celibate.'

'Rubbish,' Catherine said with characteristic bluntness.

'No, it's not. It's not rubbish. I've never understood what all the fuss is about.'

'But it can be so . . . wonderful.' Catherine's body gave a little shiver as she thought about it.

'Not for me.'

'It's fantastic with the right man.'

'I've never had the right man, then.'

'Never?'

'Never.'

'You've had orgasms, haven't you?'

'What pass for orgasms. That's not saying much.'

'Like what?'

'Well, a climax. A crescendo. But not earth-shattering. Pleasant, that's all. I could easily live without that.'

'You definitely haven't had the right man. Do you masturbate?' The frankness of their friendship had clearly not been affected by the intervening years.

'There's no point.'

'Why not?'

'Because it doesn't work.'

'So you must have tried?'

'I've tried. Nothing much happens. Do you?'

'What?'

'Masturbate?'

'God, yes, all the time.'

'And?'

'I come like the parting of the Red Sea. That's the trouble with sex. The more I get the more I want. Sometimes I have to do it twice a day. I can't stop myself. I'm good at it too. I know my body. I know what it likes.'

'Perhaps that's it, perhaps I'm just not very good at it. I wish I was.'

'Do you?' Catherine looked at her friend with an intense stare.

'What do you mean?'

'Do you really wish you could turn yourself on?'

'Of course I do,' Paula said very definitely. 'At least I think I do,' she added, with less certainty, the alcohol slowing down her capacity for rational thought.

'If you really do, I'll teach you,' Catherine said positively.

'How can you do that?' Paula said. The idea made her giggle.

'Easily.'

'Don't be silly.'

'I'm not. I can teach you if you really want to learn. But you have to want to . . .'

'I don't see how you can.'

'Trust me. Look a lot of sex is just technique. Pressing the right buttons. But it's not something anyone ever gives lessons in. If you don't meet the right man you might never find out. I was lucky. When I was seventeen I spent the summer with this family in France. The elder brother sort of took me in hand. He taught me everything. I never looked back.'

'I remember you telling me about him.'

'Well, then . . .'

'Well, what?'

'I can teach you. It's just like learning anything else. All the equipment's there Paula, believe me, you just have to learn how to use it.'

'I don't think my equipment's working properly.'

'Let's go and see.'

'What, now?'

'Why not? No time like the present. The booze has lowered all your inhibitions.'

'But . . . now?'

'Or never?'

There was a silence. Paula looked over at her friend. Catherine was not smiling. She was clearly deadly serious. For some reason this realisation made Paula's pulse race.

'OK, now,' Paula said more decisively than she felt.

'Good. Come on. Let's go upstairs.'

'Upstairs?' Paula questioned.

'Of course. It's a demonstration, not a lecture. Come on.' Catherine got to her feet and held her hand out to help Paula up. 'You look as if you're just about to go in to see the dentist.'

'That's what it feels like.' Paula could have changed her mind, of course. She didn't know how the conversation had taken such a dramatic turn, but it had and, at the very least, it would be a good opportunity to prove to herself once and for all that her body was not properly adapted for sex. Whatever gene was responsible for creating sexual pleasure was missing from her DNA. She took Catherine's hand and got to her feet.

The bedroom was large and spacious. There was a separate dressing room to one side and a small marble-lined ensuite bathroom. The king-sized bed was covered with a bright blue counterpane that toned with the dark blue carpet and pale blue walls.

Catherine turned on the bedside light then used a built in dimmer to reduce its glow to a bare minimum.

'Take your things off,' she said.

'You're serious about this, aren't you?' Paula said. The walk upstairs had sobered her up a little.

'Deadly. Come on, do as teacher tells you.'

Paula was wearing a neat but unspectacular grey jersey suit and a white blouse. She took the jacket off and unbuttoned her blouse, revealing her cotton bra. Like most of her underwear it had been washed too many times, its whiteness faded to a nondescript taupe.

'Honestly, Paula, you've got to buy some new bras.'

'I know. Never seem to get round to it.' She pulled her blouse off and wriggled out of her skirt. Catherine's eyes fell to the faded cotton knickers she wore under her tights. She raised a disapproving eyebrow but said nothing.

'Just take your tights off, for now.'

Paula felt a little self-conscious. It was not that both women hadn't seen each other's bodies hundreds of times. They had had some of their best conversations while one or the other of them took a bath. But being here under these circumstances had created a different context. She didn't let it stop her, however. Skimming the tights down her legs she sat on the edge of the bed, kicked her flat heeled shoes off, and pulled the nylon from her feet.

'Have you done this before?' she asked.

'What?'

'Taught the art of sexual self-awareness?'

'That sounds like an American religious sect! But no, I haven't. I think I know what you need, though.'

'What are you going to do to me, then?'

'Lie back and I'll show you. Trust me, Paula.'

And Paula did. She lay back on the counterpane with her arms by her sides like a patient waiting for the doctor to examine her. Catherine opened the top drawer of the nearest bedside table and took out a black silk sleeping mask.

'Put this on,' she said.

'What for?'

'Just do it.'

'All right.' Paula slid the elasticated straps of the mask around her head then slipped the padded silk over her eyes. Darkness descended and she welcomed it. She was beginning to wonder if this was such a good idea after all. Perhaps if she hadn't had so much to drink she would never have agreed to any of this. She was quite certain that Catherine's efforts would fail.

'Are you comfortable?' Catherine said.

'Yes.' Oddly, Paula thought, the silk pressing against her eyelids was a pleasant sensation, soft and sensual.

'Roll over on to your stomach.'

Paula obeyed. She felt Catherine's hand unclip her bra.

'Back again.'

Again she obeyed. This time Catherine's hand plucked her bra away.

'You always did have great tits,' Catherine said. 'I'm going to take your knickers off now.' Her hands grasped the waistband of the cotton knickers and, as Paula raised her buttocks off the bed, Catherine drew them down Paula's legs. 'You could afford to buy satin and silk, Paula. They feel so much nicer. That's all part of it.'

'What is?'

'Being a woman, being feminine. There're all sorts of sensual pleasures. You've got to become more aware of your body.'

'I've never been that interested.'

'Well, change,' Catherine said firmly.

Paula heard a drawer open, then felt Catherine's weight on the bed beside her.

'You've got such a beautiful figure, Paula, you haven't changed at all.'

Something light and soft floated down on to Paula's chest, covering both her breasts. It felt like silk, perhaps a silk scarf. The touch of it made Paula's nipples pucker with a speed she had never experienced before.

'Does that feel nice?'

'Mmm . . .'

'And this?'

The silk was dragged down towards Paula's belly. It grazed the short hairs of her pubic triangle then caressed her thighs and glided over her knees. Reversing the direction, Catherine pulled the scarf back up over Paula's breasts and hard nipples.

'That's lovely,' Paula said. She was surprised at her body's reaction. She felt a strong spasm deep inside her sex.

'Good.' Catherine left the silk covering Paula's breasts. 'Now take this.'

Paula felt something being thrust into her right hand. It was cylindrical and ribbed, though the tip of it was smooth.

'What is it?'

'Have you ever used a dildo?'

'You're not serious!' She'd always imagined dildoes as something butch lesbians used as a substitute for a penis. She felt a sharp sense of revulsion at the idea. But, strangely, she also felt an equally strong surge of excitement at the same time.

'I thought not,' Catherine said.

'What, am I supposed to shove it up me?'

'No. Let me show you.'

Paula felt Catherine grasp her wrist. She was glad of the blindfold. It provided a blessed anonymity. Not being able to see gave her the perverse feeling that she couldn't be seen either. She could never have done this with her eyes wide open. Catherine guided her hand down to the top of her thighs.

'Press it up between your legs. Lightly at first.'

'Is this what you do?'

'Among other things.'

Paula opened her legs a fraction. The touch of the silk seemed to have sensitised her body. Despite her scepticism about her ability to respond sexually, she actually felt quite aroused. Perhaps it was the booze. Perhaps it was the blindfold. Didn't they say depriving a person of one sense increased the sensitivity of all the others? Or perhaps it was something else, something she didn't want to face or even think about.

The cold, smooth plastic of the tip of the dildo nosed into her labia.

'Try and get it against your clit,' Catherine said quietly.

'I have.' That was odd too, Paula thought. Her clitoris felt nodular and swollen. Usually, even in the throes of what passed for passion, it was very slow to engorge.

'Good, now I'm going to turn it on.'

'Turn what on?'

'It vibrates. Where have you been the last hundred years?'

Looking back, if Paula had to pick a moment when her life had changed completely and utterly she supposed she would have had to pick the moment Catherine's hand reached out and turned the gnarled ring at the base of the dildo. Before, she had imagined sex was something that could be ignored, side-lined and compartmentalised. But what happened as the dildo began to vibrate against her clitoris changed all that totally, turning her life upside down.

It would never be the same again.

The sensation was so unexpected and so totally affecting that Paula moaned aloud. It was as though she had been plugged into a powerful electric current. Waves of sensation seized the little nodule of nerves, then rushed out through her body. She felt her vagina contract and her nipples throb, her nerves all combining to deliver a massive pulse of pleasure. Reflexively her muscles tensed.

'That's it,' Catherine said quietly.

'Oh, Cath . . .' was all Paula could say. She pressed the dildo against her clit more strongly. The added pleasure increased the sensation. She tried to tell herself that this couldn't be happening, that something like this, something so crude and obvious, couldn't be affecting her so profoundly but it wasn't true. Whether she liked it or not her clitoris was responding to the vibrations by sending wave after wave of pure pleasure through her whole body. She was intensely aware of the silk covering her nipples. Harder than she had ever felt them, they seemed to be rubbing against it, throbbing with the same pulse that was beating in her vagina, making it contract rhythmically. Her clitoris danced to the same tune.

She wanted to relax, to try and step back and take a breath, but it was simply impossible. She had always been the sort of person who analysed and rationalised everything that happened to her. She wanted time to stop and think and work out what on earth was going on, but her body wouldn't let her. It didn't want intellectual reasoning. It wanted sensation. Almost before she realised what she was doing her hand was moving the tip of the dildo up and down against her clitoris, producing a whole new catalogue of feelings. Her labia were wet, soaking wet. She could feel her juices leaking out of her body. She could feel, right at the core of her, a lake of wetness, as though a dam had burst inside her.

'Oh God . . .'

She actually felt scared. She was so glad Catherine was with her. Putting out her free hand, she felt her friend take it, and grip it tightly. But, like everything that was happening to her, this contact too seemed to crank up the voltage of the electric current of feeling that was running through her body.

Somewhere in the blackness behind the blindfold a little voice was telling her it was simply not possible for her body to respond with such vigour.

But it was. What was more, Paula knew she was going to come and that it was going to be like nothing she'd ever experienced before. Scissoring her legs apart, she thought she could feel her labia parting, the mouth of her vagina opening. Her vagina was still contracting wildly. It had never been stimulated like this with a man.

'Oh God . . .' she repeated, almost screaming the words this time. A huge bubble of feeling swelled up from her sex, constantly enlarging, extending further, rising higher. It engulfed her, making her eyes roll back and her toes curl and every muscle in her body stretch, as though on some imaginary medieval rack. Time seemed suspended. Perhaps it was seconds, perhaps it was hours, Paula could not tell. Then the bubble burst and she did scream. She couldn't help herself, the pleasure was so acute it was almost like pain. In the blackness she saw fireworks, incandescent reds and flicking white. Her body returned from the rigidity of steel to the softness of jelly. Her mouth was wide open gasping for air, the fire of the orgasm consuming all her oxygen.

She could do nothing for a long time but let the feelings flow over her.

'I felt it too,' Catherine said almost whispering.

'You were right! I always thought it was me, the way I was built.'

But it wasn't over. Paula didn't want it to be over. Her orgasm hadn't left her sated. Quite the reverse. She wanted more. Like a child with a new toy she wanted to play with it again. The experiment had just begun. Without saying anything else, without waiting for Catherine's guidance, knowing exactly what she wanted, Paula slid the dildo in to her vagina. It filled her. It thrust in to her. Immediately she pulled it almost all the way out then plunged it back in. Suddenly, in her mind's eye she saw a man's cock driving up into her, not any man in particular but a generic example, a hard, veined shaft, topped by a pink, smooth glans, throbbing as it disappeared into her body. This time she held the dildo deep inside her, feeling it nudging against the neck of her womb.

The sequence of feelings she had experienced before began again, like a giant wheel slowly beginning to turn. Her vagina contracted around the dildo, and her clitoris pulsed wildly, as though a fresh supply of blood was pumping into it. She squeezed Catherine's hand. In the blackness she could imagine her friend sitting beside her looking down at her naked body. She had a sudden desire to be touched by her. She wished she would cup her hands over her breasts. She wished she would hold the dildo, or caress her clitoris. That idea seemed to connect with her physical feelings to create a new surge of pleasure. She was coming again. She managed to pull the dildo out, then thrust it in once more, but as the long, broad cylinder plunged into her body she could do nothing else. She screamed, a noise so loud it startled her, and a sharp orgasm, completely different from the first, and yet essentially the same, raked through every nerve in her body. She arched up off the bed, rigid, supported only by her shoulders and her heels.

It was a long time before the orgasm had run its course and she sank back on to the bed, exhausted.

'The experiment was a success, I take it?' Catherine said.

'What happened to me?' Paula said as she sat up. The silk slipped from her breasts. She pulled the mask off and blinked. A large, cream-coloured plastic dildo lay between her legs, slicked with the juices from her body. 'I'm still shaking,' she said, holding out her hand. It was trembling. Her whole body felt different, as if she was floating, not quite in touch with the real world. 'I've never done that in my life.'

'It's just a matter of attitude. You allowed yourself to open up, that's all.'

'No, no it wasn't just that. It was that thing . . .' She gestured at the dildo. 'I had no idea . . .'

'Sometimes they're a good way to get started.'

'Have you always used one?'

'Yes.'

'When we were at university?'

'Yes. I told you I've always needed a lot of sex. I love it. That's a handy substitute.'

'I'm still having trouble understanding. I don't think I've ever had an orgasm before, Cath. Not like that. I thought I had, occasionally, but I was obviously just kidding myself. That was fantastic.'

'Come on, I'm going to put you to bed now. You need to rest.' For a moment Catherine looked at Paula's naked body. It was as though she wanted to say something, but then changed her mind. It was then Paula noticed the expression on Catherine's face, though it was not one she understood. It was, she thought, a wistfulness.

'Is there something wrong?' Paula asked.

Catherine hesitated again. Then she jumped to her feet, snapping herself out of her private thoughts. 'No, no,' she said. 'Come on, I'll show you your bedroom.'

# Chapter Two

It was a crisp, bright winter's day. The sky was blue, dotted with cloud as white as cotton wool and the air was still. It was cold, bitingly cold and breath turned to vapour as it was exhaled, but the direct sun warmed Paula's face.

She had given herself a long lunch and taken a taxi to Bond Street, where she had browsed among the shops. She hadn't bought much but, interestingly enough she thought, her previous, almost total lack of interest in clothes, had changed. Whereas before she had often bought the first thing she had seen that was in the right size, today she was much more critical of what looked good on her and what did not. She'd tried on several dresses and for the first time she had been conscious of the way they felt on her, how she reacted to the material, to its softness and sensuality. That was definitely a change, she mused, and a change for the better.

She *had* bought some new underwear. Again she was cautious, trying on more than she eventually bought, still not completely trusting the first flood of a new found enthusiasm. But in the changing room of Courtney's in Brook Street, as she tried on the silk and satin lingerie she'd selected from the racks on display, the way the beautifully supple material moulded itself to her body gave her a quite unexpected *frisson* of pleasure. The result was a hefty bill and a carrier bag containing five carefully chosen items.

She hailed a taxi on the corner of Brook Street and got back to the office by three.

'George wants you,' her secretary said as she got out of the lift on the third floor, the Courtney bag in her hand. Her secretary, Julie, didn't like her. It was not personal. Julie didn't like the world. She thought she was superior to the rest of the people in it. She was meant for better things. Her dissatisfaction that this fact had not yet been recognised was taken out on all and sundry. 'At once,' she added, like some school mistress talking to an errant child.

Paula went into her office and closed the door, wondering for the umpteenth time how she could get rid of the girl. She dumped her packages and took off her coat. The phone on her desk rang.

'Yes?'

'Paula? You're back, then.' It was George Fairbrother.

'Just. I got the message.'

'Where have you been?'

'Shopping.'

'Get up here, will you?' He sounded angry. George was the head of the mergers and acquisitions at Lichtman Terry and her immediate boss and he was not known for his equanimity.

Paula suspected she knew what was wrong. A client of the company, Robert Parker, the chairman of London Capital Conglomerates, had been working to acquire a stake in a company prior to making a formal bid. Under Stock Exchange rules he was allowed to control up to thirty percent of the share capital before he was obliged to make a formal bid. Lichtman Terry had been charged with buying up as many shares as they could under nominee ownership in order to protect his identity. Once it became known that Robert Parker was interested, the price of the shares would rocket.

Unfortunately, over the last two days Paula had been unable to pick up more than a million and a half shares, little more than half of one percent of the equity, and the share price had climbed dramatically. There could be only one conclusion. News of LCC's interest had leaked.

Paula tapped two buttons on the computer terminal on her desk and the screen came to life. The price of Winkworth's, the target company, had gone up another ten pence while she'd been out at lunch.

She couldn't help reading a certain delight in Julie's face as she headed for the lift. Other people's discomfort was a cause of satisfaction to her.

Paula got off the lift on the top floor. Fairbrother's office was at the end of the corridor, his secretary, Jean, a woman in her fifties with a matronly appearance and a kindly disposition, perched at a desk in a small ante-room outside.

'Go straight in,' she said as Paula arrived. Unlike Julie she looked sympathetic, knowing what Paula would have to face.

Paula rapped on the oak-panelled door. Though the building was modern, Lichtman Terry's interior designer had tried to give the impression of a long-standing, traditional company – which Lichtman Terry was – and all the doors and walls were panelled with reclaimed oak. Dark green predominated in the colour scheme, with fixtures in brass, and desks and chairs were all reproductions of antique designs.

'There you are,' Fairbrother said as Paula walked in. 'Glad you could spare the time to join me,' he added sarcastically.

'I was only out for a couple of hours,' Paula said, sitting in the leather wing chair in front of his Victorian partner's desk.

'It's a bloody disaster,' Fairbrother said.

He was a short, fat man, bald with a round head and small

features. His body was round too. He looked like a cricket ball balanced on a beach ball. His eyes bulged from their sockets as though he had a thyroid problem and his complexion was on the red side of pink.

'Winkworth's, right?' Paula asked.

'Of course, Winkworth's. The shares are up fifty pence this morning.'

'There's obviously been a leak,' Paula said calmly.

'Obviously. The point is, where's it come from?' He was looking at her accusingly.

'Not from me,' Paula said sharply.

'How can you be so sure?'

'There has been no leak from my office. I am the only person who knows who is behind the purchases and I certainly haven't told a single soul. I'm not taking the blame for this, George.'

'Where then? Robert Parker is one of our biggest clients, if not the biggest. If he can't trust us to be competent enough to pick up a stake in Winkworth's without attracting this sort of attention, he'll go to some other firm. Do you know what that would do for our turnover?'

'I can imagine.'

'Well, you'd better find a way to prove to him that it was nothing to do with us. With *you*. Do you understand? I should never have put you on this.'

Paula railed at that. 'Why not?'

'You haven't got enough experience.' Fairbrother didn't approve of women in business. He would have loved to find an excuse to have Paula fired.

'That's ridiculous. This has nothing to do with me and you know it. Nothing I've done has leaked. I don't know why the share price has gone up but it might be totally unrelated to our share deals.'

'Pigs might fly.'
'I'll find out what's happened.'
'You better had. Parker's back from Budapest on Friday.'
It was Monday. She had four days to find an answer.
'Get on with it then,' he said gesturing for her to leave.

As Paula closed her front door, the phone rang. Dropping the Courtney's carrier bag in the hall she ran into the sitting room to answer it.
'Hello.'
'Paula. Catherine.'
She had not spoken to Catherine over the weekend. She had sent her a card thanking her for dinner and carefully refraining from mentioning her gratitude for the far more important event. She had found it so difficult to understand what had happened to her that after three days the whole episode had assumed a dreamlike quality.
'Hi, I've been meaning to ring you.'
'Listen, can I ask you a favour?'
'Anything?'
'Are you busy tomorrow night for dinner?'
'No.'
'The thing is, Doug's got a big deal on at the moment...'
'I bet.' All Latimer's deals were big, Paula imagined.
'Anyway, he's asked this guy out to dinner.'
'What guy?'
'The one he's doing a deal with. Some new process for solar power. This guy's from Bombay. I was telling Doug about you and he wondered if you'd like to come and make up the numbers. It always makes things a bit more relaxed if it's a foursome. Would you?'
'Of course.'
'Great. I'll come round at seven.'

'Seven. That's a bit early for dinner isn't it?' Paula protested.

'I've got a present for you.'

'What sort of present?'

'I'll see you at seven. Thanks. Bye for now.'

Paula put the phone down. She went into the kitchen and poured herself a glass of red wine. Curiously, she thought as she brought the glass to her lips, her hand was trembling slightly. She knew what had caused it – the sound of Catherine's voice.

Taking the wine with her, she picked up the Courtney's bag and went upstairs to her bedroom. She turned on the bath taps and, as the water ran, emptied the contents of the carrier bag on to the bed. She had never spent so much money on lingerie in her life. Each item, wrapped in white tissue paper was of black silk, inset with lace. There was a bra, a pair of French knickers, a pair of thong cut panties and a short slip. Most extraordinary of all, for her at least, was a suspender belt. She couldn't remember the last time she had worn stockings. She thought it had been at the wedding of her cousin when she was thirteen. She'd worn frilly white garters to hold them up. She wasn't at all sure why she'd bought the suspenders and the black stockings to go with them. The shop had had a photograph of a model in the whole set of lingerie and there was something about the way the black stocking tops had made the girl's thighs look – soft, creamy, vulnerable – that might have been the explanation for Paula's impulse buy.

Finishing the wine Paula stripped off her clothes and got into the bath, wallowing in the warm water, sinking down into it until only her head was above the surface. For the whole weekend she had deliberately tried not to think about Catherine and what she had done. Her subconscious, however, had had other ideas. She'd dreamt about her twice. The first time Catherine had been standing on the corner of the wide tree-lined avenue where she lived, dressed in a black satin skirt and a red satin blouse. The blouse had been unbuttoned to display Catherine's large breasts, pushed into a deep cleavage by a white lace bra. A car, a large, sleek yellow car, had stopped and Catherine had leaned down to talk to the driver. Next thing Paula knew she was in the back of the car and Catherine in the front giving the man a blow job while he drove. She seemed to be able to speak at the same time as she was telling Paula that it was going to be her turn next and she should climb over into the front seat.

The second dream was the same, except this time Catherine was naked and the car had stopped in some field or park. Catherine was bent over the bonnet while the man took her from behind. She kept telling Paula to get ready because he wanted to have her too. Paula had realised she was naked except for a silk scarf tied around her breasts. When the man had finally finished with Catherine he had pulled out of her and turned to Paula, who saw that instead of a cock the phallus that jutted from his loins was a cream-coloured plastic dildo.

Obviously these dreams were her way of trying to digest an experience unlike anything she had known before. But there was something more fundamental they had not, apparently, touched on and something she had been avoiding. Catherine's voice had reminded her of it, a painful reminder she almost said to herself. She suspected that her sudden explosive orgasms had only been partially to do with the magic properties of the vibrator. That had certainly contributed, but she couldn't help wondering if it would have had such a powerful effect if Catherine had not been on the bed beside her. She remembered how she had imagined

Catherine looking at her naked body and how the touch of her hand had affected her so strongly. The truth was, at that moment, she had wanted to do more than touch Catherine's hand.

Paula had never felt that way about a woman before. Never. She had never harboured the slightest sexual inclinations towards women. That was why it had come as such a shock to her to realise that, as the first really proper orgasms had raked through her body, it was images of Catherine, distinctly sexual images, that were playing in her mind.

What she could do about it, what she should do about it, Paula had no idea. But just the memory of lying there on Catherine's bed had made her nipples pucker and her sex moisten. Casually she rubbed the palm of her hand over each of her nipples. She felt an instant and surprisingly strong throb of sensation. Her nipples seemed to have developed a neural pathway to her clitoris that had certainly never been there before. It throbbed too. Unbidden, an image of Catherine's face popped into her mind.

Scolding herself for being so prone to fanciful exaggeration, she climbed out of the bath and dried her body on a big white bath towel, hoping the vigorous motion would rub away the more delicate sensations.

It didn't. If anything her nipples grew harder. She walked back into the bedroom self-consciously, glancing at her naked body in the mirror. Her nipples crested her high, round breasts. She caught a glimpse of her face. Its expression was quizzical. What did she intend to do now? it asked.

Paula extracted the black silk slip from the white tissue paper. It had a scoop neckline and spaghetti straps. The silk felt incredibly soft. She rubbed it against her cheek then pulled the garment over her head, raising her arms and letting it fall over her body. The silk cascaded over her breasts. She had felt that sensation before, as Catherine had pulled the silk scarf across them. For the second time that night her clitoris throbbed so strongly it made her catch her breath.

Her feelings were ambivalent. She was torn between ignoring her feelings and exploring them. She wasn't at all sure she wanted to find out what it would feel like to touch herself. On the other hand her body was already responding with little thrills of sensation she could not remember experiencing before.

Reluctantly, almost, she threw the rest of the lingerie to one side and lay on the bed. The movement caused the silk to rub against her nipples again. Her breasts and nipples seemed to have been tenderised. They reacted to the caress of the silk with a huge wave of feeling. Her nipples were so hard they were plucking at the rest of the flesh of her breasts, pulling it as tight as a drum skin. She closed her eyes. There, in the darkness Catherine was waiting for her. In her mind's eye she could see her drawing the silk scarf over her breasts, though she had not been able to see her doing it in reality. Her clitoris felt as though it were alive, wriggling against her labia.

Catherine again. Damn. She didn't want to think about Catherine. Paula cast around for a masculine image to replace the spectre of her friend, but she couldn't think of any single instance of sex with a man that had been nearly as exciting as what had happened with Catherine. Her hand ran down the soft black silk. Its smoothness was positively sensual. She caressed her thighs, parting them slightly so she could run her hand down the inner surfaces. Her clitoris was like a thing possessed, pulsing wildly, determined to draw attention to itself.

Paula pushed her finger down into her labia. It butted

against her clitoris almost by accident and she felt a shock of sensation as though it had been touched by a live electric current. It had never responded like this. It was big too, exactly like it had been the other night, swollen and distended. Gently she rubbed her finger against it. Again she felt an unexpected thrill of pleasure. She didn't understand what was happening to her. The last time she had masturbated her clitoris had remained soft and unresponsive, barely registering any sensation let alone this almost overwhelming intensity.

There was no point in fighting it any more. As she stroked her finger up and down the little nut of nerves she replayed the whole scene. She remembered it all graphically. The way she'd taken off her skirt and blouse under Catherine's critical gaze. The way Catherine had handed her the silk sleeping mask and how it had felt pressing against her eyelids. Then the incredible jolt of pleasure she experienced as the vibrations of the dildo shot through her clitoris. But she was struggling to remember something else. After it was all over. The way Catherine had looked at her after it was all over, that was it. The look in her eyes, that wistful look in her eyes which had suggested, however fleetingly, that Catherine's interest in her friend's naked body was more than purely objective. The idea made Paula's heart pound. Could it be true?

The gentleness had gone. She was rubbing hard now, pressing her finger down on to her clit. She saw Catherine standing by the bed, stripping off her clothes, unclipping her bra, freeing her heavy breasts, stepping out of her panties . . .

'No . . .' Paula said aloud, hoping the voice would scare the phantom away, not wanting Catherine there but at the same time wanting her more than she'd ever wanted anything sexually before.

'What are you doing?' Catherine's imagined voice said.

'Can't you see?'

Her finger was strumming her clitoris like a string of a double bass. Her whole body was wired, stretched across the bed, every sinew tight. Her body had always stubbornly refused to respond to her efforts at masturbation before but now it was reacting with unqualified vigour. She knew she was coming. What's more she knew it was going to be as intense an orgasm as she'd had with Catherine. The pulse of energy from her clitoris was as regular as clockwork, but each surge was stronger and more affecting.

'I want to kiss you,' she imagined Catherine saying, 'on the mouth and on your pussy.'

'No!' Paula cried.

The pulse quickened. It was so fast now it had become one continuous flood of feeling. In an instant the flood became a torrent. It picked her up, wrung her out then dropped her back on to the bed again, breathless, exhausted and replete.

She raised her head and looked down her body. It was as though it belonged to someone else. The two points of her nipples stuck up under the black silk like the tips of tent poles under canvas. Her hand was still pressed into her thighs. She pulled it away and closed her legs creating a tremor of feeling as her clitoris was trapped between her labia again. It was like the aftershock of an earthquake. Which, in a way, it was, she thought. The earth, after all, *had* moved for her. She laughed out loud at the thought.

But the laughter died away. As she sat up and the sense of physical pleasure began to drain away, it was immediately replaced by worry. She had never experienced an orgasm like that by her own hand before. It was exactly like the orgasms she had had with Catherine. The problem was they had all been occasioned by Catherine, either in person, or incorporeally by virtue of Paula's fevered imagination. It was not a difficult equation to work out. For the previous years of her sexually active life she had been with men, her sexual energies directed towards the heterosexual. Suddenly, after all that time, circumstances had led her to an encounter – an entirely one-sided and very limited encounter admittedly – with a woman. It had caused her to respond with an ardour and passion she had thought herself incapable of. Ergo, it was not the dildo or a sudden unaccountable change in her physical metabolism that had been responsible, but the fact that her desires had been directed at a member of her own sex.

Paula Lindsey had to come to terms with the fact that she might be a lesbian.

'Something to drink?'

'Mineral water. Tynant. Sparkling,' he said to the waiter.

'Same for me,' Paula said.

'Certainly madam.' The waiter hurried.

They were in a large modern restaurant, the decor minimalist. The floor was black slate, the walls white, hung with abstract paintings in primary colours. The sculptured and uncomfortable chairs were stained in the same red, yellows and blues of the pictures. The food was minimalist too, and arranged on the plate with the same impulse that had inspired the painter of the abstracts. Unfortunately it did not taste as good as it looked. But it was Justin's choice. He liked it here. She suspected he liked it because most of the waiters were gay, and Justin had recently come out.

'So?' he said.

'Winkworth's,' she replied.

'Fantastic, isn't it? Did you go along then?'

'No.'

# THE WAYS OF A WOMAN

'Pity. I took a new position at the start of the account. Very lucrative. Let's say my Christmas bonus is assured.'

'Did you get a tip?'

'Why are you so interested?' The fact that he didn't know confirmed for Paula that no lead had come from Lichtman Terry. Justin wouldn't have asked that question if he already knew she was trying to buy up the company.

'I can't say. But I need to know.'

'Well, they're definitely in play.' That was city argot for a company that was about to be the subject of a takeover.

'Obviously. But who?' Paula had no intention of tipping her hand.

'The rumour is it's Ideal Nation.'

'That's absurd. Ideal got burnt in manufacturing two years ago. They've sold off all their plant. Why would they want to go back into it again? Besides they've just bought Ketman's and their gearing is too high for another acquisition. If they went for Winkworth's their share price would plummet.'

The waiter arrived with the dark blue bottle of mineral water. He poured it into two tall glasses primed with ice and lemon.

'Thank you,' Paula said.

'Madam.' He walked away.

Justin Brooks was her oldest friend in the world in stockbroking. They had been trainees together at a merchant bank. At the end of the course Paula had been offered a job by Lichtman Terry, Justin had stayed with the bank.

'So you don't believe the rumours, then?' His smile suggested that he knew the truth.

'No. Come on, Justin . . .'

'You can't use it, Paula. We'd both lose our jobs.'

All city firms were carefully monitored, all trades on the

markets carefully logged. Any unusual activity leading to large profits were investigated, the use of information gained as a result of working inside a company or one of its associates, strictly illegal.

'I don't want to use it for a position. I'm not mad. I need to know for another reason.'

'What reason?'

'You can't use what I tell you either,' she warned.

'Of course not.'

'I need to know to keep my job.' She explained briefly about Fairbrother's accusation and her interest in Winkworth's shares. She didn't tell him that she was acting for Robert Parker and he didn't ask. It was better to avoid temptation.

'All right, but this mustn't go any further. We act for Blinkman. He's got a twenty percent stake in Winkworth's. He's been approached to sell it by Klein.'

'Alma Klein?'

'Exactly.'

'God.' That made perfect sense. Alma Klein was the head of a large conglomerate in New York. Her avariciousness when it came to buying up other companies was well known. It meant, almost certainly, that Winkworth's had a capacity that would fit neatly with her own and would be used for rapid expansion in one particular division of her business. But, off hand, not knowing Klein's business profile that well, Paula could not think of which.

'You can't use this,' Justin repeated.

'I won't. At least I know.'

'It's not going to make much difference is it?'

'What do you mean?'

'Well, if you tell Fairbrother he's not going to believe you without proof. He'll think you're just picking a name from the air.'

'You're right. When . . .' she was just about to say Robert Parker's name. She corrected herself, 'when our client gets back on Friday, he's going to be out for blood. Unless Klein makes a bid before then and goes public, Fairbrother will put the blame on me. I could be out.'

'Do you know anyone who knows Klein?'

'No. I don't think so.'

The waiter arrived with two large white plates. Delicately arranged on each was a rocket salad, a tiny pile of chopped red chilli and a circular tomato galette.

'You'll think of something,' Justin said cheerfully.

'I'll have to,' Paula said, though for the life of her at the moment she could not think of what.

For the first time in all the years she had known her, Paula was not looking forward to seeing Catherine. The truth was she was scared, frightened of what her reaction to her would be. She had thought a lot about her in the last twenty-four hours. Much too much. As hard as she'd tried, in every spare moment she'd found herself dwelling on her friend and the problem she had come to represent.

In the years they had lived together, Catherine had never given her the slightest hint of any sexual interest. They had frequently slept in the same bed when another friend had come to stay, and often walked around their flat in the nude without any embarrassment. Paula was positive Catherine had never shown the faintest interest in her body. But perhaps, she thought, that was because she hadn't recognised it, because the idea of anything but friendship between them would have seemed totally alien to her.

Besides, Catherine had always been very definitely into men. At university, and in the flat they'd shared later, there had been a parade of them, in every shape and size. In all their late-night confessionals, as Catherine revealed the details of her experiences with them, telling Paula graphically what they had or had not done to her, and what they had wanted her to do to them, she had never once mentioned any interest in the distaff side. Which is why Paula told herself she was simply imagining that the look she had given her on Friday night was anything more than a casual glance that, in her emotional state, she had misinterpreted. It had not meant, and did not mean, Catherine wanted to take her to bed.

The trouble was, the more she convinced herself that she *was* imagining things, the more confused she became because she could not decide whether this was a relief or a disappointment. In the watches of the night, it was a disappointment, in the bright light of day, a positive relief. Now, as seven o'clock approached and the thought that Catherine would breeze in as if nothing had happened was uppermost, it was a disappointment again.

It was ten-past seven when the dark blue Mercedes parked a little way down the street. Paula watched from her front window as Catherine got out of the car, locked it, then took a large red box from the boot.

'Hi,' Paula opened the door before Catherine could ring the bell.

'Good evening.' They kissed on both cheeks.

'What's that?' Paula pointed at the box as Catherine walked inside.

'I told you. It's a present.'

'I've got a bottle of champagne on ice in the sitting room,' Paula said.

'Great.'

Catherine walked into the front room and dropped the parcel on one of the armchairs. She looked around. 'This is really nice. Very you. All those books.'

'You had wardrobes, I had bookshelves, remember?'

Paula had set an ice bucket on the coffee table. It was an offer *Moët et Chandon* had promoted. Buy a case and get a free ice bucket in the shape of a top hat. The case had long been drunk and the bottle in the ice bucket was now Lanson Black Label. She poured the wine, feeling her pulse race as she handed a glass to her friend.

Catherine was wearing a tight red body under a short, pleated skirt. Her tights were opaque black lycra, the sort of material that was shiny and incredibly tight. Her shoes were black too and had a spiky heel.

'Cheers,' Catherine said sitting on the small two-seater sofa in front of the fireplace where Paula had lit a small log fire. 'This is cosy,' she said nodding at the fire.

'One of life's little luxuries. Can I open my present?'

'I had an ulterior motive. This place we're going to tonight is *trés* posh. I thought you might not have the right *accoutrements*.' She said the last word in a French accent. 'Don't worry, Doug can put it down as expenses.'

Paula was not insulted. Catherine had lived with her long enough to know her taste in clothes was purely functional. She pulled the top off the box and searched among the multiple folds of tissue paper. She held the dress up.

'It's sensational!' she said. The dress was the most beautiful dark violet colour, with a plunging neckline, a cinched waist and a tight, short skirt. It was belted in the same material with a large buckle in gold that looked like a coiled snake. 'What a fabulous colour.' Paula's hand caressed the material. She was surprised that her reaction to its silky softness was quite physical. Her nipples stiffened. 'I'll go and try it on. What time are we expected?'

'Nine.'

'Will you help me?' Paula asked. Was that a loaded

question, she wondered? Was it just an excuse to get Catherine into her bedroom? Her heart was beating so fast she could hear it in her ear-drums. She was sure she was blushing. Hopefully Catherine would think it was just her excitement at the dress, but Paula's reaction to her friend had been quite unequivocal from the moment she had touched her lips to her cheek. A hard knot had formed in her stomach. Though she had rarely, if ever, experienced such a feeling, she couldn't mistake what it was. It was lust.

'Of course,' Catherine said, getting to her feet, her skirt bunching up, Paula found herself noticing, around her thighs. 'I'll bring the champagne.'

Paula led the way upstairs, the red box under her arm, while Catherine brought the ice bucket and glasses.

It was curious, Paula thought, as they walked into the bedroom, that though Catherine was her best friend, the person she knew better than anyone else in the world, at that moment, she felt like a perfect stranger.

'Love the bed,' Catherine said, stroking the brass bedstead. 'Good leverage,' she added, smiling.

'I kept it to remind me of Andy.'

'Oh, this was the one you found him handcuffed to, was it? With the hooker?'

'The very same.'

Catherine sat on the edge of the bed and put the champagne on the bedside chest. 'Come on, let's see how it looks,' she said. 'I'm sure I got the size right.'

Paula headed for her bathroom. She was suddenly embarrassed to strip off the track suit she was wearing in front of her friend. She was wearing the new black silk bra and thong cut panties and, in her over-active imagination, thought that might be making too obvious a statement. She couldn't bring herself to close the bathroom door for the same reason. After so many years of being so open with each other, a sudden coyness would be obvious, she thought.

She stepped into the dress and zipped it up. The material hugged her body. It suited her perfectly. She had never seen herself looking like this, the dress creating an air of elegance and sophistication. She couldn't decide whether it was the image in the mirror, or the feeling of the sensual material clinging to her body, or the fact that Catherine was next door, but whatever the cause, her sex was distinctly moist and her nipples as hard as little chips of marble.

Paula strode back into the bedroom.

'*Voilá!*'

'Hey, that's great!'

Paula pulled her hair up so it was off her neck. 'With my hair like this? Yes?'

'Definitely. You've got that lovely long neck. Like a gazelle. You're really gorgeous Paula. I could never understand why you didn't make more of yourself.'

'You know I was never interested in clothes.'

'I know. But it's time you started. There's more to life than work.'

'What about these?' Paula fished out a pair of black suede high heels from the back of her wardrobe and squeezed them on to her feet. They had been an impulse buy at a sale and she'd never worn them. They were practically the only pair of high-heeled shoes she owned. The rest of her collection was low or flat-heeled.

'Perfect,' Catherine declared, refilling her champagne glass. 'You *shall* go to the ball.' She propped herself on the pillows, kicked off her shoes and put her legs up on the bed.

'It makes me feel different,' Paula said twisting around in front of the mirror on the bedroom wall. The heels shaped and firmed the muscles of her calves. She had good ankles, the Achilles tendons pinched on either side of the heel bone. She was intensely aware of her body. Her nipples were so hard she was surprised they weren't poking through the dress. The silk of the lingerie and the material of the dress seemed to caress her flesh, setting her nerves on edge.

'Do you have any decent knickers?' Catherine asked. 'I mean judging from the other night . . .'

Paula felt herself blushing again. 'As a matter of fact I went on a little shopping expedition.' She pulled open the top drawer of the chest of drawers and pulled out the black French knickers she'd bought.

'La Perla. Very nice,' Catherine said.

'I bought the whole set. I've got the rest on.'

'Let me see.'

It was the most natural remark in the world. Hundreds of times before, they had paraded for each other in various newly purchased items of clothing, though, in truth, it had more often been Catherine than Paula. There had never been any embarrassment. But the agenda was different now, at least as far as Paula was concerned.

'Unzip me, then,' Paula said trying to keep her voice steady. She came over to the bed and turned her back on her friend. She heard the long zip sing as it was pulled down, and felt the tight material giving up its grip on her body. Pushing the shoulders of the dress down, she let it fall to the floor. She stepped out of it, picking it up and draping it carefully over the top of the chest of drawers.

'Wow!' Catherine said. 'What a difference.'

The bra was cut low, its cups designed to raise the breasts and push them together. The soft flesh of Paula's full breasts billowed out of the black silk. The panties were no more than a wide band of material that tapered down to her crotch, then emerged again from the top of the cleft of her buttocks.

# THE WAYS OF A WOMAN

The silk was so transparent the equilateral triangle of her pubes was clearly visible.

'It's a new experience for me. I bought a suspender belt too.' She knew Catherine frequently wore stockings. When they'd lived together she had made fun of her for wearing anything so uncomfortable and old-fashioned. But Catherine took the teasing with an enigmatic smile. 'You should see the effect they have on men,' Paula remembered her saying.

'You wearing stockings! Wonders will never cease.'

'I thought I'd try. Not with that dress though. It's too short.'

'What's got into you?'

'Isn't it obvious?' Paula sat on the edge of the bed beside her friend. She reached for her glass of champagne, and sipped it.

'Not really,' Catherine said.

'If you really want to know the truth, it's all to do with the other night.'

'Really?'

'I'd never had sexual feelings like that, Cath. They took me by surprise.'

'It's just a question of attitude. You opened yourself up to it, that's all. You've always been so focused on your career, you've never allowed yourself time to—'

'It's not just that,' Paula interrupted, touching Catherine's arm. Her pulse was racing faster. 'I mean, you're right. I know that. I've always put that side of my life on hold. But what happened last week . . .' Was she actually going to be able to come out with this and tell Catherine what she felt?

'Go on.'

'Cath, we've always been frank with each other, haven't we?' She put her hand on her friend's leg. The shiny lycra was silky to the touch.

'Yes.' Catherine looked puzzled, not able to guess what was coming next.

'This is hard for me to say.'

'Do you think I did the wrong thing, Paula? Perhaps I shouldn't have used the dildo . . .'

'No. No. Not that. It's just . . .' Her voice trailed off as she struggled to find the right words. She didn't want to offend Catherine and lose her friendship. 'You know I've always been very sensitive to atmospheres, to little nuances of feeling.'

'Yes.'

'Well, when we were together I seemed . . . I felt . . .'

'What?'

'That you wanted to go further. Am I way off the mark?'

Catherine sat up slightly. Her face gave nothing away. 'You mean that I wanted to touch you?'

'Not just touch.'

Catherine picked up her champagne glass and sipped the wine. It was a moment that seemed to last forever as far as Paula was concerned.

'And if I did?' Catherine said putting the glass down again. 'How would you have felt about that?'

'If you'd asked me that a week ago I'd have said, without any doubt, that I would have wanted to run a mile. Now I'm not so sure. Are you going to tell me the truth?'

'The truth?'

'Did you . . . do you want me?'

Catherine laughed gently. It was a light, pleasant sound. 'Paula, of course, I do. I always have. You're beautiful.'

'Always?' Paula looked astonished at that.

'Well, not at the beginning. I didn't tell you everything that happened to me at university. Do you remember me going out with that Swede?'

'In the second year, the one with the very blond hair?'

'Yes.'

'You never said much about him.'

'He was much older than us but he was just incredible in bed. I mean, the best I'd ever had. God, the way he made me feel. And he could do it for hours.'

'And?'

'He was married. After the first four or five times he asked me if I'd mind meeting his wife.'

'What on earth for!'

'His wife was only a couple of years older than me. It didn't seem so clear cut at the time but looking back I realised they had done it before.'

'Done what?'

'Shared the same lover.'

'You went to bed with both of them?'

'Eventually. At first he told me she just wanted to watch, said she'd got this thing about watching him with another woman. I thought it would be exciting. And it was. She just sat in a chair by the bed and the way she looked at us was a real turn on. But, of course, it didn't stop at that. After the second or third time, she asked me if I'd mind if she touched me. It just seemed like such a natural thing to do. And then I discovered I liked it. More than liked it. You know I was always into sex. This just seemed like a natural extension of what I was already into. One night she asked me to go around to their house and Sven wasn't there. We went to bed together, just the two of us. It wasn't better than with him. Or worse. It was the same intensity, but different. After that . . .'

'You went to bed with other women?'

'Yes.'

'Why didn't you ever tell me?'

'Because we were living together very amicably and I

thought you'd be uncomfortable if you thought I was constantly imagining what it would be like to get into your Marks and Spencer cotton knickers.'

'Were you?'

'Not constantly. Sometimes. I'm not a lesbian. I guess I'm bisexual. I love sex. I'm very highly sexed. I need a lot of it. As far as I'm concerned sex is sex. Sleeping with women was a good alternative to sleeping with men and it was easier.'

'Easier?'

'Not so many complications. Men find it difficult to accept sexually aggressive women. But I could walk into a gay bar and pick up a woman without an eyebrow being raised.'

'Is that what you did?'

'Occasionally. When the need arose.'

'I had no idea.' Paula's heart was pounding. Her fingers seemed to have become glued to Catherine's leg.

'So, to answer your original question, yes, I did want you last week. Seeing you lying there with that dildo jammed between your legs made me feel very randy. I had to use it myself as soon as you'd gone to bed.'

'But you didn't say anything.'

'We'd only just met again. As far as I knew you're straight. I didn't want to spoil our friendship.'

'The thing is . . .' Paula said hesitantly.

'What?'

'I don't think I am. Straight, I mean.'

Catherine laughed that good-humoured laugh again. 'And what do you base that on?'

'Because I haven't been able to stop thinking about you, or that night. Because when I came I was thinking about you and when I did it again last night I couldn't help imagining we were together. I've never had orgasms like that with a man.'

'So you think you're attracted to women?'

'It's logical, isn't it?'

'Sex isn't very logical. It might just be I pushed the right buttons, at the right time. It might just have been the dildo. You said you'd never used one before. I've known other women who've been very strongly affected by them.'

'There's only one way to find out, isn't there?' Paula said. They had cleared the air. Now Paula knew Catherine had taken female lovers before there was nothing to stop her from pursuing matters further. It was not going to offend her friend. It would not alter their friendship even if the experiment was a failure. Paula took Catherine's hand and pulled her up into a sitting position. The expression on Catherine's face was quizzical, one eyebrow raised. Paula brought her lips to within a few inches of Catherine's mouth. She had never done anything as bold as this in her life. She looked at Catherine's fleshy mouth and felt what she could only describe as a surge of desire.

'Are you sure you want to do this?' Catherine asked.

Paula answered by moving forward, touching her lips against those of her friend, not kissing them but just moving her head slightly from side to side, so they brushed against each other. 'Help me,' she said without moving away.

'No, you've got to do it.'

Paula knew she was right. She had to take the initiative, not merely allow herself to be seduced. She pushed her mouth forward tentatively and slid her tongue into Catherine's mouth. It felt so different from any man she'd ever kissed, meltingly soft and sensuous. She could smell Catherine's musky and expensive scent.

'Mmm...' Catherine moaned by way of encouragement.

The kiss became stronger. Paula ran her hand up to the back of Catherine's neck so she could press their mouths together. She felt their tongues dancing against each other.

'Well,' Catherine said, pulling back and holding Paula at arm's length. Her eyes were sparkling with excitement. 'Is it what you imagined?'

'I don't know. It's so different.'

'God, this is making me randy.' She got to her feet and picked up her handbag. Taking out a tiny portable phone, she flipped it open and punched in a single number. The phone's memory did the rest.

'Doug,' she said, into the phone after no more than a couple of seconds. 'We're running late . . . does it matter? Oh right, well I'm in bed with this gorgeous blond with the biggest cock you've ever seen and I've promised to give him a blow job before I leave. Is that what you wanted to hear? No, I don't know how late. We'll be there as soon as we can. Take him to the bar and give him a drink. We'll be worth waiting for, honey, promise.' She blew a kiss into the phone, pressed the END button, and dropped the instrument back into her bag. 'Well . . .' she said, smiling.

## Chapter Three

'Well . . .' Catherine's whole body had changed, her face softening, her hips undulating almost imperceptibly. 'This is going to be interesting.' She reached behind her back and unzipped the short skirt. It dropped away. The gusset of the body cut deeply into her crotch. She wriggled the red material over her shoulders and down to her ankles, then straightened up. The fabric of the body had been tight enough to provide support for her breasts so she wasn't wearing a bra. Paula had seen her breasts before. They were like two large melons, heavy and ripe, but, despite their weight, they defied the forces of gravity and were not in the least pendulous. Their nipples were small in comparison, and the surrounding areolae no more than the thinnest band of dark brown. Her legs were long and slender, the lycra tights following every contour.

'You're beautiful,' Paula said. She was seeing her friend through different eyes, as though seeing her body for the first time. The surge of desire she felt as she looked at Catherine's breasts was an entirely new experience for her; it felt surprisingly natural. She tried to remember if she had felt the same thing when she'd looked at a man's erection. She came to the conclusion that she had not.

'Come here,' she said. She caught hold of Catherine's hand and pulled her towards the bed, opening her legs so she could stand between her knees. She dipped her head slightly, wanting to take the initiative again and, with a growing feeling of excitement, sucked Catherine's left nipple into her mouth. She sucked it hard. She didn't know what she was supposed to do, how she was supposed to make love to a woman, so all she could do was try to think of what she would like to have done to her. With the edge of her teeth she sawed across the tiny bud of corrugated flesh, then pinched it quite hard, moving her hands up behind Catherine's back and caressing her generously fleshed, lycra-covered buttocks. The shiny lycra made the movement frictionless, letting her hands slide sinuously over it.

'Lovely,' Catherine said.

Paula gripped the waistband of the tights. As she transferred her tongue over to the right nipple she wriggled the tights down to Catherine's knees. She felt Catherine's body tremble as she pinched her nipple in her teeth again.

'Let me,' Catherine said. She pulled away, sat on the edge of the bed and stripped the tights off her legs. She wasn't wearing panties.

Paula stared into her lap. Catherine's pubic hair was blonde. Instead of growing in a triangle it was shaped like a long, fat cigar.

'I've never done this before. I don't know what to do. Will you help me now?' Paula said. She had done enough to prove she was responsible, that all this had been her idea.

Catherine turned to her, one hand resting on her thigh, the other moving up to the clip of the black silk bra. She undid it and used the same hand to pull the cups away from Paula's breasts. As Paula extracted her arms from the shoulder straps Catherine rubbed her palm against each nipple in turn. 'Take your panties off,' she said softly.

Paula got to her feet and pulled the silk panties down her long legs. They were both naked now. It was a relief that she had been right about the way her friend had been looking at her, that it was not just a product of her over-active imagination.

'What, now?' she asked. It was extraordinary that in all her sexually inspired musings about being with Catherine she hadn't for one second thought about what they would do, about the mechanics and geometry. She had imagined their bodies pressed together and their mouths locked in a kiss but nothing else. What did lesbians do? She didn't have a dildo and didn't think Catherine carried one in her handbag everywhere she went.

Catherine smiled. She lay on the bed. 'Come and lay beside me, here,' she said patting the bed.

Paula obeyed. As she lay down Catherine rolled on to her side and raised herself on one elbow. 'Perhaps I should blindfold you again,' she said with an impish grin.

'No, I want to see you.'

'That's good.'

Catherine kissed her lightly on the lips. Her hand ran down over Paula's navel to the triangle of short hair. 'You really are beautiful, Paula. I'm glad this has happened. I was having real trouble keeping my hands off you the other night, watching you lying there, writhing around with that dildo.'

'Were you? I didn't know. Not until the end.'

'Open your legs,' Catherine said, rolling on to her side.

The words excited Paula. She spread her legs apart. She knew her sex was wet and wasn't sure whether she should be embarrassed by it or not. She felt Catherine's finger slip between her labia. It found her clitoris unerringly, pressing it hard against her underlying bone.

Paula moaned. Her body clenched with a shock of sensation so strong it was almost as if she was about to come. She tried to wrestle herself back under control.

Catherine's finger began to rub more gently in a circular motion.

'Nice, isn't it?'

'Wonderful.'

'Men are good for some things, women for others . . .'

No man had ever felt like this. Men had touched her clitoris, but never with such exquisite delicacy. It was responding with massive waves of pleasure, as intense as any the dildo had produced. She looked down at Catherine's voluptuous body, one of her large breasts resting on her own, and felt a sharp pang of lust.

'Catherine . . . what's happening to me?'

'Just relax.'

'If you keep doing that I'm going to come,' Paula said.

'Good. That's what I want. Do it for me this time. Let me see it.'

'Yes . . .' That made sense. She wanted to show her friend how she could respond. She wanted to touch and feel Catherine too, but that would have to wait. The pleasure that was rolling through her body was simply too strong to fight. Catherine's finger was on exactly the right spot, stroking it with exactly the right rhythm. 'Catherine . . . Catherine . . .'

The words were strangled by the crescendo of feeling. Her body shook and her eyes closed. Her orgasm was sudden, but not unexpected. It was a release of tension, of emotional tension as much as physical. In her mind's eye she saw Catherine's nakedness. The image provoked and extended the feelings. She snapped her head to one side, then back to the other, her body rigid. Then, slowly a thaw set in, her muscles softening. That sensation was almost as pleasurable as the orgasm itself.

It was true, she thought, as soon as she was capable of

thinking again. She was a lesbian. Half a minute of being in bed with another woman, the slightest of touches, and she had had an orgasm more intense than the sum of all the orgasms she had ever experienced with a man. The enigma of her sexuality had been solved.

But, for the moment, she put such thoughts aside. Exactly as had happened on Friday night, her first orgasm had left her hungry for more. What was even more extraordinary, after the years of striving for pleasure, after the disappointments and frustrations she had endured, was that she was absolutely confident that she could come again. In fact, she knew, the trouble was going to be controlling the feelings and not letting them engulf her.

Paula rolled on to her side so she was facing Catherine. 'That was so good,' she said before kissing her hard on the lips, not at all tentatively now. She pushed her body forward and experienced a huge jolt of sensation as her breasts were crushed against her friend's. Her nipples had never been as sensitive, reacting almost as strongly as her clit.

Breaking the kiss, Paula slid her mouth on to Catherine's throat, licking and sucking at her flesh while she used her hand to roll her on to her back. She moved her mouth lower, kissing the flesh of her breasts then attacking her nipples, mashing them, one after the other, between her lips. But they were not her main objective. Her mouth left the big, spherical breasts and headed into the valley between them, kissing the soft, smooth skin with little nibbling kisses. Lower still, it travelled across the flat plateau of her belly, inches away from the little copse of her pubic hair.

Paula's heart was pounding. She saw Catherine's thighs open. She could smell her heady, sweet scent, now mixed with the unmistakable, musky aroma of sex.

Very slowly, trying to control the enormous desire she

felt, she worked her mouth down over the cigar-shaped patch of pubic hair. She found herself staring into Catherine's sex. She had seen her nude countless times and had caught glimpses of her labia, but never like this, open and exposed. Her nether lips were largely hairless, and were very thick and rubbery. Catherine opened her legs wider and Paula saw her labia part to reveal the little pink bud of her clitoris and the scarlet mouth of her vagina, glistening with its own wetness. The sight gave her another strong jolt of pleasure. She had never realised before how the soft folds of a woman's body could be so desirable.

Paula came up on to her knees, then bent forward over her friend and snaked her hands under her thighs. Catherine co-operated, bending her knees so her thighs were raised. Then Paula kissed her labia fully and firmly, kissing them as though they were a mouth, squirming her lips against them. She could feel their wetness. Catherine moaned. Still not sure exactly what was expected of her Paula drew back slightly and plunged her tongue inward and upward until she could feel it butting against the swollen nut of Catherine's clit.

'Oh, yes,' Catherine said softly.

Catherine's body changed perceptibly, her muscles tensing, an underlying pulse growing stronger. But her reaction was matched by Paula's. Kneeling like this, Paula's clitoris was trapped between her labia and she could feel it throbbing.

She knew what to do now. It was like an instinct buried so deep in her psyche it had been completely hidden, even from herself. But now it had surfaced. Gently she stroked the tip of her tongue against Catherine's clit. She had never felt this part of a woman's anatomy before. Even her own clitoris, after the years of neglect, was something of a stranger to her, so she found this fascinating as well as terribly exciting. It was much longer than she'd imagined and shaped like an almond, with a distinct ridge of hardness right at its centre. Her tongue explored it, noting the geography, marking the little spots where Catherine's body reacted with a spasm of pleasure.

'Beautiful,' Catherine whispered. Her abdomen was undulating subtly. Paula adopted the same rhythm. She was getting bolder too. As she tongued Catherine's clitoris, she moved the fingers of her right hand over the back of her thighs until she could feel the plump wetness of her labia. Wriggling them forward she nudged them into the maw of Catherine's vagina. It was hot and wet. She pushed forward.

'Yes . . .' Catherine said, wanting the penetration.

Paula slipped two fingers into the hole. Another new experience, another rung on the ladder of sexual awareness. As she felt the tight tube of Catherine's vagina part to admit her, its walls silky soft, like velvet that had been soaked in honey, her own vagina clenched with delight. She loved the way the flesh seemed to cling to her fingers, contracting around them. She thrust them up as deep as they would go, straining the tendons of her hand until they were entirely buried.

'I'm . . . you're making me . . .' Catherine breathed huskily unable to finish the sentence. Paula's tongue and fingers were too affecting. Her whole body began to shake uncontrollably and Paula felt her clitoris twitching. Catherine moaned loudly, as if trying to form a word, then shuddered profoundly, like a ship going aground, every part of her responding to the enormous implosion of feeling Paula had created.

But Catherine's climax, like Paula's before her, left her energised and hungry for more. If she had any doubts about her friend, if she'd wanted to take it slowly so as not to scare her, or trample on her burgeoning feelings, such thoughts were driven away by a rush of passion. She pulled herself down the bed until her head was level with Paula's knee.

'Like this now,' she said, looking up at her friend, then tugging on her leg to indicate she wanted her to swing it over her head. 'Together.'

Paula did not hesitate. She whipped her leg over Catherine's shoulder and boldly, like everything else she had done in the last few minutes, pressed her sex down on to Catherine's mouth. At the same time she pushed her own face between Catherine's thighs again and drove her tongue deeper into her labia. The impact of both actions was like a hammer blow. The softness of Catherine's mouth against her sex, her tongue immediately probing for her clitoris, was matched by the feeling of her mouth on Catherine's sex. Nothing had prepared her for this. The one sensation seemed to feed on the other. Catherine responded as she nudged her tongue against her clitoris again, more than doubling the pleasure she was experiencing as Catherine did exactly the same thing to her.

It was seconds, perhaps even less than seconds, before she felt her body racing to orgasm for a second time. As she reached under Catherine's thighs and jammed her fingers up into her vagina again, she felt Catherine doing exactly the same thing to her. As her nipples rubbed against Catherine's stomach, she felt Catherine's rubbing against hers. Everywhere she looked and touched there was a sexual stimulation she had never experienced before. It was wonderful, breathtaking, orgasmic. She tried to concentrate on giving Catherine pleasure, not for any altruistic motive, but because she realised the more she felt Catherine wriggling and writhing on top of her, the more pleasure she got. She could feel every spasm of ecstasy in Catherine's body. And there were many of them, erratic at first, but very soon establishing a rhythm as strong and regular as a heartbeat. It was a rhythm that matched the tempo of her own body.

She had been right. There was no doubt about it now. She was a lesbian. Her efforts with men had all been wasted. This is what she wanted, because this is what she was. She could glory in women, wallow in their softness and sensuality.

Catherine's clitoris was twitching and her sex was contracting around her fingers. But Paula's clit and her vagina were doing the same. It was perfect.

As her orgasm broke, as she gave in to a flood of exquisite pleasure, higher and more profound than the first, she pushed her lips hard against Catherine's sex and knew she was coming too. Their bodies were locked together, rocking wildly against each other like a boat tossed on a stormy sea, hugging each other to extract every last ounce of feeling.

Gradually the winds relented, their orgasms dying down, the rocking motion subsiding to a comforting and almost imperceptible undulation.

Eventually Paula rolled off her friend.

'Why didn't we do this before?' she asked. Then they both started to laugh.

'Darling, so sorry we're late.'

Catherine walked into the bar. She was wearing a slinky black dress with a long, full skirt that was split to mid-thigh and a sweetheart neckline cut low enough to reveal a great deal of her pneumatic bosom, blossoming out of a lacy black bra. They had driven to Catherine's house for her to change, then taken a taxi to the restaurant. Fortunately, it was only around the corner, so further delay had been kept to a minimum. In fact they were exactly one hour late.

'Doug Latimer,' Catherine continued after she had kissed

her man on both cheeks, 'this is Paula Lindsey.'

'Nice to meet you, Paula,' Doug said. He was of medium height with broad shoulders and a body that, if not exactly slender, was not, as yet at least, running to fat. His hair was a dark brown and thick, greying at the temples. He had a rather long face with a complexion etched with deep worry lines. His mouth was small with thin lips and he had dark brown eyes that looked at Paula critically, moving from her face to her shoes then back up again.

A tall and very handsome man had got to his feet with Doug. He was probably the same age as the banker, which Paula estimated to be in the region of early fifties, but he looked much younger. He had silky black hair, a rugged face and a slender, lithe body, his olive-skinned complexion more Mediterranean than Indian. His dark brown, almost black, eyes sparkled with an unmistakable mischievousness, their whites the colour of the purest snow. He reminded Paula of the captain of an Asian cricket team. 'This is Ranji Patra,' Doug said, introducing him to the two women.

'I'm delighted to meet you,' he said extending his hand and shaking Paula's. His fingers were long and bony with long black hairs on the back of his hands and between the knuckles. His grip was firm. His eyes looked at her steadily and she could see he approved of what he saw.

'You've met Catherine, before, of course,' Doug said.

'Of course.' Ranji took Catherine's hand and kissed it. 'You are looking your usual exquisite self, Ms Bidmead. I gather you had a domestic crisis. Nothing too serious I hope.'

'Domestic problem?' Catherine looked bemused.

'Your heating system,' Doug said, prompting Catherine with the excuse he'd made up on her behalf.

'Oh, yes. Right. No heating. In this weather it's not funny. Sorry we're so late. No choice but to wait for an engineer.

Didn't want to get back to a cold house.'

'No, absolutely not.'

'It's all fixed now.'

They were sitting in a large bar outside the main restaurant. It was decorated in plush reds: dramatic scarlet walls, deep red carpets and a gilded cornice and elaborate plasterwork on the ceiling. The comfortable armchairs were upholstered in pink, clumped around large, gilt coffee tables. An empty bottle of champagne sat in front of them in an ice bucket and the waiter was summoned to bring a fresh one and two more glasses.

'Cheers,' Catherine said with determined jollity, ignoring the waves of annoyance at her lateness which were emanating from Doug.

'Indeed,' Ranji said raising his glass and looking at Paula.

Paula sipped the wine and tried to relax. After what had happened to her earlier, going out to dinner was the last thing she had wanted to do. She would have preferred to stay in bed, husbanding the extraordinary feelings Catherine had created, and digesting the emotional impact of what it all meant to her. She wouldn't have minded at all if Catherine had stayed with her, to kiss and cuddle and cosset her, and, no doubt in time, repeat the whole circle of events. She felt her body shudder involuntarily at the thought.

'Are you cold?' Ranji asked, spotting the shiver. His eyes hadn't left her for a second.

'No, no. Just someone walking over my grave,' she replied.

'I'm sorry?' Ranji looked alarmed.

'It's an expression we have in England.'

'Meaning?'

'I'm not sure. It's used to cover those little shivers we all get.'

'Of course. In India we do not have this expression. May I say that this dress is a most beautiful colour.'

'Thank you.'

'Shall we order?' Doug said irritably. 'Or it'll be the small hours before we eat.' He aimed the remark at Catherine. 'We've read the menu backwards as it is.'

'I'd like grilled Dover sole and a green salad,' Catherine said blithely. 'I've got to watch my weight.'

'It looks as though you have succeeded admirably in this endeavour,' Ranji said.

'How charming,' Catherine replied.

The *maître d'* arrived on Doug's signal and took their order, Paula following Catherine's lead, not really in the mood for food. A few minutes later they were escorted to their table in the large ornate dining room, its style something of the Belle Epoque, with stained glass windows and more red plush. The round tables were set with pink linen table cloths and surrounded by Louis XIV style dining chairs. Highly polished silver and sparkling crystal glasses reflected the flickering light from the silver candelabra on each table, and the firelight from a huge log fire set in the middle of a gothic fireplace which dominated the room.

They chatted easily, Catherine soon thawing the frost of Doug's anger. It was curious, after everything that had happened earlier in the evening, that the more Paula talked to Ranji, the more attractive she found him. He had an ease and grace about him that suggested he was a man who had come to terms with himself and he moved with an economy of gesture that fascinated her. His eyes had a way of crinkling at the corners when he smiled that Paula found endearing. His smile was also infectious. She found it impossible not to smile back.

Had Paula not discovered, only a few hours earlier, that

she was wasting her time with men, she would have undoubtedly been very interested in Ranji Patra.

'How long have you known each other?' he asked nodding at Catherine, who was talking animatedly to Doug.

'Since university.'

'Really,' he looked surprised at that. 'You went to university?'

'Is it unusual for women to go to university in India?'

'No. Well, not if you are wealthy.'

'Why are you surprised, then?'

'I just . . . sorry, I was making an assumption that is quite unwarranted.'

Paula didn't understand that, but let it pass.

'Do you mind if I tell you that you are quite lovely. Your eyes, your figure . . .' He looked down at her body, his eyes dwelling on her bosom.

'No,' she said. 'I can take a compliment.' But there was something about the way he was looking at her she didn't understand either, as though she in some way belonged to him. She put it down to cultural differences. Perhaps Indian men had got into the habit of looking at women proprietorially.

The funny thing was that this intense stare excited her. She knew that couldn't be the case, of course. She knew what she was probably feeling was a transference of the enormous sea of emotions she'd felt earlier. She was not excited by this man's quite obvious attraction to her. It was merely a backwash of feeling from the arousal Catherine had created.

As they waved away the sweet trolley and ordered coffee and a bottle of *Suduiraut Sauternes*, Paula caught Catherine looking at her. It was a far from objective stare and Paula felt her body respond with a jolt of equal desire. If she had any doubt about the effect Ranji was having on her, it was immediately dispelled. Nothing he had made her feel matched this. She wondered if it were possible for Catherine to dump Doug and come back to bed with her? Bearing in mind Catherine's financial dependency on her companion she thought it unlikely.

It was one o'clock when Doug called for the bill. He settled it with an American Express Gold Card then hustled them out of the restaurant, explaining that he had to be up early in the morning. They were the last to leave and by his firm grip on Catherine's arm it didn't look as if they were going to be parted for the rest of the evening.

It had been an odd dinner. Though Ranji had paid a great deal of attention to her, Paula had hardly exchanged a word with Doug, even though, as they both worked in the City, they had a lot in common. She certainly knew several of his employees, and he, no doubt knew George Fairbrother and Aaron Lichtman. She realised that neither men had even asked her what she did for a living. With the current state of play at Lichtman Terry she was glad not to bring the subject up, but she thought it strange that there hadn't been even a passing reference to the subject. Perhaps, she thought, she was being hypersensitive. After what had happened earlier in the evening she was expecting the dinner to be a bit of a trial. Actually she had enjoyed it, largely due to Ranji.

'Would you mind if Ranji takes you home, Paula?' Doug asked outside on the street.

'Of course not,' Paula said.

'Sorry, darling,' Catherine whispered as she kissed Paula's cheek, 'duty calls.' She winked suggestively.

A black Rolls Royce Silver Wraith had drawn up to the curb outside the restaurant. The chauffeur hurried to the passenger door and opened it.

'Call me,' Catherine said, as she climbed in.

'Goodnight,' Paula said.

'Nice to meet you,' Doug said climbing in too. 'Bye Ranji. Take good care of her, now.'

'Don't worry, I will,' he said.

The car drew away. Catherine waved through the back window.

'Taxi, sir?' the uniformed commissionaire asked.

'Thank you.'

A black cab appeared immediately. They climbed into the back. 'Royal Mews Hotel,' Ranji told the driver, making no attempt to ask Paula where she lived.

She was just about to protest but stopped herself. She realised she didn't want the evening to end. It had been a little like a dream. Her body felt as if it were floating, suspended on invisible strings, not really in contact with the real world. She didn't want to go home and face her empty house and the rumpled bed. That would bring all the memories flooding back and she would be forced to face the consequences and implications of what she had done. She wanted to delay that for a little bit longer at least.

'Are you kidnapping me?' she said.

'Of course. Has Doug taken care of all the details?' Ranji asked.

Paula didn't know what this meant. Perhaps he hadn't seen Doug paying the bill in the restaurant. 'I'm sure he has,' she said.

'Good. I prefer it that way.'

'What are we going to do?' she said.

'Oh nothing out of the ordinary,' he replied hastily.

'What deal are you doing with Doug?' They hadn't got round to that over dinner.

'I'm a research scientist. You know Doug runs an

investment bank? He's going to finance the manufacturer of a new solar energy cell I've developed.'

'Sounds interesting.'

'It is. But not on a night like tonight.' He looked out of the window. There were stars in every square inch of the sky and the slenderest of crescent moons. 'In India,' he said, 'there is little light pollution. You can see stars right down to the horizon, as if they were falling off the edge of the world.'

The taxi drew up outside the hotel. Another commissionaire hurried to open the taxi door and they got out. Ranji paid the driver then slipped the commissionaire a ten pound note too.

He took Paula's arm and guided her inside. There was a large bar to the left of the foyer, with six or seven people sitting in little groups, but Ranji ignored it and walked her over to the lift.

'Are we going to your room?' she said, without the slightest alarm in her voice.

'I've got a suite,' he said, as if that were explanation enough.

Paula supposed she could have said no. It would be easy to get the commissionaire to hail her another cab. But she didn't want to. She wasn't worried. She felt protected by her new status as a lesbian.

The lift took them to the second floor. On any other night Paula might have wondered why he hadn't even asked her if she'd like a nightcap, let alone whether she wanted to come to his room, but tonight her brain wasn't functioning properly. It had been overloaded with too much stimulation. It needed rest and recuperation and a large brandy.

Ranji guided her down the corridor to the door of his suite. He took a card from the inside pocket of his smart grey suit and swiped it through a slot at the side of the doorjamb. The lock buzzed loudly and Ranji pushed the door open, then stepped aside to let Paula go through first.

'You really are beautiful,' he said as he closed the door after them. 'Would you like a drink?'

'A brandy,' Paula said. Paula certainly felt beautiful. She had all evening and that was a new experience too. The silk lingerie and the dark violet dress made her feel quite different. She had always scoffed at women who insisted on spending their time and money on clothes but now she was beginning to see that there was something to it after all. She was only too aware of the way men had been looking at her all evening, the heads that had turned as she walked into the restaurant, the waiter's eyes on the neckline of the dress, the taxi driver watching her in his rear view mirror. It had never happened before and it felt good. But it wasn't just the effect they had on the outside world. The point she had missed was the effect they had on *her*. She was sure that her acute awareness of the way the silk seemed to caress her body was only a temporary phenomenon. Her body had been tenderised by her experience with Catherine, every nerve set on edge. She had never spent an evening, as she had tonight, being so conscious of her sex and her clitoris, and her nipples. Every time she moved she swore she could feel the silk of the bra, or the crotch of the tiny panties, pulling against her oversensitised erogenous zones. Her nipples were permanently hard, like chips of marble, and her clitoris was pulsing so much it felt like a tiny animal burrowing around at the top of her labia.

'There's your brandy,' Ranji said. He had gone to the long sideboard in the sitting room of the suite and poured her a large glass of Otard XO.

'Aren't you having one?'

'What do you say in England? "I'm driving".' He seemed to think this was funny. Paula could not understand why.

The sitting room was lavishly decorated, the walls lined with herringbone beige material, the floor carpeted in thick oatmeal wool. The lamps and armchairs and two small sofas, as well as the cushions that littered the seats, were all upholstered in differently patterned cloths, in different colours, though they all subtly blended together.

'Excuse me for a minute, will you?' he said.

'Of course.'

Ranji opened the double doors that led to the bedroom and then closed them behind him.

The brandy was smooth and delicious. It made Paula feel slightly more in contact with the real world. She wandered round the room. There was a wall-to-ceiling bookcase in one corner stacked with leather-bound books. She browsed through them, finding editions of H.G. Wells and Thomas Hardy.

'There. Didn't take long.'

Paula had assumed he'd gone for a pee. In fact he'd taken all his clothes off and was now naked apart from a very small towel which was precariously knotted around his waist. His body was powerful and athletic, his abdomen lined with muscles, his arms bulging with firm, well-developed biceps and triceps, his thighs hard and contoured too. His chest was broad, the intercostal muscles of his rib cage delineating each bone.

'I prefer a blow job usually, but in your case I think I'll make an exception,' he said sitting on one of the sofas.

Paula was so astonished she was at a loss for words. He took her look of surprise to mean something else. 'That is all right, isn't it? You said Doug had taken care of everything. He usually does.'

'What do you mean?' she managed to blurt out.

'I mean, he has paid you, hasn't he? I wouldn't like there to be a misunderstanding.'

'*Paid* me?' Paula's mind was groping around for some explanation to cover this set of circumstances.

'Yes. He said it was all his treat. Is something wrong? It's all right. If he fucked up I've got some cash in the bedroom.'

The penny suddenly dropped. Doug Latimer, in common with several other businessmen, must be in the habit of oiling the wheels of commerce by providing some of his associates with call-girls. For some reason he'd forgotten to tell Ranji that Paula was not of that fraternity. She started to smile. The smile turned to a grin. Now the initial shock had worn off she felt flattered. No one had ever mistaken her for a call girl before. In her ankle length skirts, polo neck sweaters and flat heels that would have been highly unlikely. But flattered was not all that she felt. She seemed unable to take her eyes off Ranji's body. He was the sort of man, strong, rugged and exotic that she had always dreamt of going to bed with, and had never once got near. The effect he was having on her was marked. She found she had developed an almost irresistible desire to rip that small white towel off his body and see if his cock was as well developed as the rest of him.

It was ridiculous, of course. She was a newly confirmed lesbian. She had proved to herself that men had no interest for her. They simply did not turn her on.

'Is something wrong?' he repeated looking worried.

'No,' she said without really thinking what she was doing. 'Nothing's wrong. It's just that you're so . . . strong.'

'I work out a lot. I like to keep fit.'

'You've got a fantastic body. I don't think I've ever seen

a man so well developed.' It was perfectly true. Her husband had been overweight and flabby. Most of the men, no, *all* of the men she had been to bed with had been far from perfect physical specimens. But Ranji was an Adonis. He could have modelled for an anatomical map of the muscle groups of the human body. 'Do you want me to take my clothes off?' What was she saying? She must be mad. She was being stupid. Just because he resembled a Greek god, he was still a man, and men were of no interest to her anymore. The trouble was, her body seemed to feel differently. As she looked at Ranji she felt a strong physical desire. It was, she realised, that transference again, confusing what she had felt earlier for Catherine with what she was feeling now.

'Mmm . . . I've been looking forward to this all evening, I have to tell you. I'm afraid I spent most of the meal trying to imagine what you were wearing under that enchanting dress.'

Paula stood in front of him. Her heart was beating like a drum. With a calmness she did not feel and a motivation she did not fully understand she unzipped the violet dress and pulled it off her shoulders, wriggling it down her hips. She couldn't have been more perfectly costumed for the role in which she had been cast. The La Perla black silk bra struggled to contain her full, firm breasts. The thong cut panties nestled under her very sheer black tights. Had she known she was going to be acting out the part of a whore she wished she'd worn the stockings and suspender belt too.

'I love black,' Ranji said, his eyes roaming her body greedily.

The dress dropped to the floor. Paula picked it up and draped it over an armchair.

There was something freeing about being cast as a prostitute, Paula thought. She didn't have to conform to any tight social conventions as to what a woman was supposed to do or not to do. She could be outrageous. In fact, that was expected of her. In different circumstances she might have found that exciting. She was excited now, her sex moistening, and her nipples pulling on the flesh of her breasts, but that was because of what she had done with Catherine, not, she knew, because of what she was doing now.

She sat down on the sofa beside him. She had never done anything as rash in her life, but she turned towards Ranji, flipped the corner of the towel up and grasped his cock. It had already started to engorge. She squeezed it hard with her fist. She usually felt intimidated and incompetent in such circumstances but tonight she was not herself. She was playing the part of a call-girl who knew precisely what to do.

'What were you saying about a blow job?' she said as she lowered her face to his lap. His cock was circumcised, the glans pink, the shaft a much darker brown than the rest of his body. She put out her tongue and tapped it against the top of his glans. His cock jerked in her hand, hardening rapidly. Opening her lips she plunged down on it, forcing it into the back of her throat. She sucked and felt it pulse.

'Lovely,' he said.

'So big,' she said pulling back so that she could look at his erection. It was long and thick, the shaft below the glans much smoother than she'd ever seen before. She felt her clitoris pulse though she knew, of course, it was only remembering Catherine's artful touch.

Ranji ran his hand down her back, under the waistband of her tights and panties. His fingers pushed down into the cleft of her buttocks until they were touching her labia. She was wet.

'Let's go into the bedroom,' he said.

'Not yet,' she said. She got to her feet. Whenever she'd

been to bed with a man before she'd always been cowed and timid, never quite sure what was expected of her. But she knew what was expected of her tonight. 'Pull my tights down,' she said standing directly in front of him.

He grasped the waistband and wriggled the sheer black nylon over her hips and down to her knees. Supporting herself with a hand on his shoulder she raised her legs, one by one, so he could pull the nylon clear of her feet.

'Now my panties,' she instructed boldly. What was she doing this for? Why was she wasting her time? Why didn't she just tell him the truth and go home? Her bedroom would still smell of Catherine's scent. She could roll around on the sheets where they had been together and replay the whole wonderful experience while she masturbated. Her sex clenched involuntarily at the idea.

Ranji leant forward. Very slowly he pulled the panties down over her hips. The narrow gusset was peeled away from her crotch. The silk whispered against her thighs. The panties fell to the floor and she stepped out of them.

'Beautiful,' he said staring at the neat triangle of short brown hairs that all pointed inward and downward. 'So neat. As if you comb them.'

'I don't.'

Paula felt his eyes boring into her, his face level with her crotch. She looked at his cock. It stuck up from his lap at right-angles, a tear of fluid escaping from his urethra. She wanted it. She wanted it inside her. She was transferring her new sexual feelings for Catherine to the more accustomed sexual object of a male erection. Perfectly logical if you knew your psychology, which she did as she'd read it at university as part of her multi-disciplined course. It was her body's way of coming to terms with its new orientation. After a while this transference would fade and she would no longer feel attracted to men at all. At the moment however, she had an overwhelming desire to impale herself on that large totem of masculinity. And, playing the part in which she had been cast, she could do just that.

Paula spread her legs and straddled Ranji's knees. She inched forward until the tip of his cock was almost touching her labia. She looked down, sure she could feel juices running out of her body and down her thighs.

'Very hard,' she said.

'It's throbbing.'

'Would you like to see my tits, now?' She couldn't remember when she'd ever used the word 'tits'. She reached behind her back and unclipped the black bra. Like a professional stripper she held the cups to her breasts with one hand and peeled the straps off with the other. Finally she tossed the bra aside then shook her shoulders from side to side to make her breasts slap into each other, right in front of Ranji's face.

His eyes sparkled with excitement. He stared at her breasts, watching them until they stopped quivering. Then he looked up into Paula's face. 'You're really something,' he said.

'Is this what you want?' she asked.

She bent her knees. His cock butted into her labia and was immediately anointed by her wetness. She angled her sex forward so his cock nudged against her clitoris. It responded with a sensation that made her gasp. Paula hadn't expected that. She wasn't sure what she had been expecting. Her clitoris felt incredibly sensitive. She moved her hips back and forth minutely so his cock stroked against the little nut of nerves and felt a surge of pleasure. What was happening to her? Was the explanation transference again? Was she imagining Catherine touching her? Or perhaps it was simpler than that. Perhaps her clitoris was raw, sensitised by overuse. Her nipples were pulsing and her vagina contracting. She wanted to feel that big sword of flesh forcing its way inside her, even if she couldn't understand why.

It was Ranji's turn to take the lead. With a speed and agility born of his obvious strength he caught hold of her hips, pushed her to one side, sprung to his feet and whipped around behind her. Bending her forward, his erection dived into the cleft of her buttocks and slid down to the mouth of her vagina, riding up into it on the flood of her juices.

Paula was taken by surprise. She had no time to intellectualise what she felt, no time to persuade herself of the reasons for the sensations that hit her like a hammer blow. She could do nothing but feel.

Ranji's hands gripped the top of her hips. With all his considerable might he pulled her back on to him as he drove his cock forward. It plunged right up into her. Paula had the extraordinary sensation that he had broken through some secret barrier in her sex. She felt her vagina opening for him, like a blossoming flower, allowing him where no man had been before. She cried out in shock as the assault was converted to a pulse of sharp, exquisite pleasure. Even with everything she had experienced earlier in the evening, she had never felt anything like it before.

Ranji pulled back until his cock was almost out of her then rammed it in again, using his hands to pull her on to him at the same time. It went even deeper, breaking new ground, his glans rearing up into her. The trouble was, there, in the newly exposed depths of her vagina, she had nerves that felt as though they had never been touched before. They reacted to the intruder with a wave of feeling like nothing Paula had ever experienced before.

But then that was true of everything she was feeling. No

man had ever filled her like this. No man had ever thrust into her so strongly. No man had ever held her in a grip of steel like this. No man's abdomen had ever felt so adamantine as it butted against her bottom. What is more no man had ever provoked the orgasm that Paula knew now was inevitable. As Ranji plunged forward, Paula felt her labia stretched apart by his breadth. This, in turn, stretched her clitoris, its wild pulsations pitched into a higher key, sending signals, and receiving them from every nerve she possessed. Her whole body trembled, her hands clutching at the seat of the sofa for support. She thought she was going to fall over but as she came he held her, sensing her need, pushing into her but not pulling back again, just squirming himself deeper as her orgasm flooded over her. It was exactly what she needed. No man had ever done that.

It wasn't the end, only the beginning. Ranji allowed her orgasm to run its course, but as soon as she felt her body relax he pulled out of her, spun her round, and picked her up effortlessly in his arms. With one arm under her neck and the other under her knees he carried her through into the bedroom.

Paula's state of arousal was already extreme. This only made it worse. It was what she'd always dreamed of, wasn't it? Being carried, being ravished. She realised that was what Ranji was going to do to her, had already done to her. It was ravishment.

'Kiss me,' she said, throwing her arms around his neck. She smothered his face with kisses, then sucked on his mouth passionately. All thoughts of Catherine were vanquished, her preconceptions wiped away. She didn't care. She didn't care about anything except what was happening to her. She felt his tongue plunge into her mouth just as his cock had plunged into her sex minutes before. It felt hot and wet and hard, just like his cock. Her body quivered. She knew she had never been as aroused as this.

'I thought you didn't like kissing,' he said.

'I love it,' she replied not knowing what he meant. How could he think she didn't like to kiss? Then she realised it was a generic 'you' meaning prostitutes. 'I love it with you,' she said quickly. Now was not the moment to tell him the truth.

He lowered her to the bed. 'You're very good at this,' he said laying on the bed beside her.

'So are you.'

'I bet you say that to all the boys,' he said laughing.

'No, I mean it.' She tried to convince him with her eyes that it was true.

He kissed her again lightly on the lips, then cupped her breasts in his hand, one after the other, pinching her nipples. Her body seemed to have racked itself up into such a state of sensitivity that she swore she'd climax again if he did nothing but that. The marvellous thing was, she knew he had no intention of just doing that. He appeared to have infallible instinct when it came to knowing what she wanted. She could feel his erection pressing into her side, hot and sticky. She wanted it back inside her.

And she got what she wanted. Ranji rolled on top of her as she scissored her legs apart. His cock stabbed down between her legs and, with the same unhesitating accuracy he had displayed the first time, reared up into her vagina.

From that moment on, it was difficult for Paula to keep track of what was happening. Her body was so unaccustomed to the shocks of pleasure that coursed through it she could barely cope with them at all, let alone remember how and why they were caused. She knew she had come again almost immediately, as she had wrapped her arms around his broad, muscled back and hugged him to her, his whole body as hard as the cock impaled inside her. She knew she'd come again only seconds after that, in the same position, as she'd experienced the same feeling he'd created earlier, his glans opening her, breaking through a secret barrier to the very core of her. But after that it was as though her body became so prone to pleasure, so used to climaxing with the greatest of ease, there was no limit to what it could do. One orgasm followed another, each different and distinct, and yet essentially the same.

He turned her on to her stomach and took her on all fours. He lay on his back while she knelt above him and rode up and down on him. He pulled her on to her back again. Every new position produced new sensations, delved into parts of her vagina that had not been touched before, manufacturing an orgasm unique unto itself.

Finally, she supposed, her body must have been sated. She simply could not come anymore. He seemed to sense it. He pulled out of her and knelt by her side, his cock in his hand.

'I want to show you something,' he said, his hand moving up and down his long shaft.

'Show me what?' she said. She watched with total fascination as he manipulated his big, wet cock. It had given her so much unbelievable pleasure she looked at it with an almost religious adoration.

'I'm going to come over your tits,' he said.

Her body shuddered at the thought. It was a wonderful idea. She couldn't think of anything she wanted more. His hand pumped up and down faster, as she scrambled closer to him, positioning her chest immediately under his cock. She didn't know how he'd managed to hold out for so long, but it was obvious now that he had decided to give into his own needs. She could see the veins in his cock pulsing. His eyes were staring at her body, moving from her face to her breasts, and down to her legs.

'For you,' he managed to say between clenched teeth as an arc of white liquid spattered down on Paula's body, hot and sticky, most of it over the proud curves of her breasts. A gob hit her right nipple. She writhed with pleasure. Had she not come so many times already, the feeling would have made her come again. A second wave, less intense, shot out too and she saw a third dribble out of him as his hand milked his phallus, wanting to extract every last drop.

# Chapter Four

'Barry? It's Paula Lindsey.'

'Paula, how are you?' Barry Howard replied.

'Not good. I need help.'

'Fire away.'

Paula stared out at the rather dismal view from her office window. While the top floor enjoyed views over the city, the third was closed in on all sides by towering blocks of glass.

'I need to get information about thermal insulation.'

'Now, what on earth do you want that for?' Barry asked.

'A new project I'm working on. Can you help?'

'Not off hand. Let me think about it.'

'There's something else too,' Paula said.

'Shoot.'

'Do you know how I could get to Alma Klein?'

'The New York Alma Klein?'

'Yes. Do you know anyone over here who works with her? It's worth lunch.'

'Dinner.'

'Lunch.'

It was an old routine between them. Barry Howard was happily married but liked to pretend that all he wanted in life was to run away with Paula Lindsey. He would have run a mile if she'd ever suggested he could get his wish.

'All right, lunch,' he said reluctantly.
'How's Mary?'
'Fine. How's your love life?'
'No comment,' Paula said, smiling to herself.
'As good as that?'
'No comment.'
'I'll see what I can come up with.'

They exchanged goodbyes. Paula looked at her watch. She had an appointment with George Fairbrother at three and it was five-to now. She had spent all morning on research, reading through all the published material on Klein Industries, and ringing anyone she knew who had ever had any dealings with the company. She had thoroughly researched Winkworth's too, trying to find the reason why Alma Klein should be so interested in a company which apparently had so little synergy with her own. On the surface there wasn't a single reason for Klein Industries to want to take over Winkworth's. But, if Barry Howard confirmed what she had discovered buried in a small article on one of Winkworth's research and development projects, she thought she might have stumbled on the reason. If she was right she could develop a strategy which would not only prove to Robert Parker that she had nothing to do with the share price movement, but provide London Capital Conglomerates with an even bigger prize. The problem was that it might be a big 'if'.

Reluctantly Paula trudged out of her office, ignoring her secretary's badly concealed glee at her discomfiture. Julie, like everyone else in the office, knew she was in trouble.

Upstairs, Paula waited outside Fairbrother's office.
'He's been in with Lichtman,' Jean told her.
'About Parker?'
'I think so.' A light on her telephone console blinked out.

'You can go in now. Don't let the bastard get you down,' she added in a whisper. It was small comfort to know George Fairbrother was universally disliked at Lichtman Terry.

Paula knocked on the door and went in.

'Well?' Fairbrother said immediately. He was standing by the window looking out. There was a thick blanket of cloud in the sky and the sort of gloomy light that was sometimes the portent of snow.

'I'm still working on it,' Paula said.

'It's Wednesday,' he reminded her.

'I can tell you it was nothing to do with us.'

'*You*,' he said gruffly. 'I told you to come up with an explanation.'

'I have.'

'So?'

'Winkworth's is the target of another player.'

'Clap-trap.'

'Alma Klein is going to mount a bid.'

He laughed. 'You have to be joking. What possible interest could Klein Industries have in Winkworth's?'

'I don't know. That's what I'm working on.'

'It's rubbish.'

Paula stood her ground. 'It is not rubbish. I know it for a fact.'

'Can you prove it?'

'No. Not yet.'

'No, of course you can't. The idea is ridiculous. Alma Klein! What did you do, pick a name out of a hat?'

'Klein is involved. She's been buying up shares in New York. That's why the share price has gone north.'

'Well, you'd better prove it by Friday or you will be out of here on Friday afternoon. And I would start looking for an alternative means of employment. I can personally guarantee that no one in the square mile will hire you. Is that clear enough?'

'Perfectly.'

Fairbrother waved her away with his small chubby hand.

'There's a visitor to see you,' Julie said, giving the impression that she couldn't understand why anyone would want to see Paula. 'I'm going home,' she added to make sure Paula's visitor was not used as an occasion for more work.

It was five minutes to five. Barry Howard had called back with a lot of information about thermal insulation processes. It confirmed all Paula's best guesses. The problem was that if her strategy was to work she would need to get in to see Alma Klein, or someone very high up in Klein Industries, and pitch her idea to them. Barry Howard had drawn a blank on that score.

There was a rap on her office door.

'Come in.'

The door opened and Catherine swept in.

'Hi. I was passing your way so I thought I'd drop by.'

'Catherine!' Paula felt a lurch of excitement. She was sure she could feel herself blush.

'Have you finished?'

'Just.'

'Have you got a couple of hours? I've been invited to the opening of a new shop. It sounds great. Beauchamp Place. Lot of new designers.'

'Well, you know I've developed a sudden interest in clothes.'

'Exactly. Bring your gold card.'

Catherine was wearing a short black suit under her wolf-skin fur coat. 'I've got my car outside. Your commissionaire's looking after it for me. He's a sweety.'

'He's a bit old for you. Come on let's go.'

Downstairs, Lichtman Terry's commissionaire, a wiry, ex-army sergeant, was guarding Catherine's Mercedes as if it were his own. He rushed to open the driver's door as Catherine walked out of the revolving doors.

'All safe, Miss,' he said.

'You've made a friend for life,' Paula joked as she got into the car.

'At twenty pounds a throw, I should think so,' Catherine said, starting the engine.

The car was warm and comfortable, its suspension soft enough to be soporific. Paula closed her eyes, the tension of the day making her feel tired.

Catherine drove fast but well, spotting the gaps in the traffic and squeezing the big sports car through them. 'Hard day?' she asked sensing Paula's mood.

'Very.'

She hadn't spoken to her friend during the day. She had been too busy and even if she had spared the time she wouldn't have known what to say. She hadn't sorted out her emotions yet. When she finally got home from Ranji's hotel it was late and she'd collapsed into bed and fallen into a deep and apparently dreamless sleep. She hadn't found a moment since then to try and work out what she felt or didn't feel, and how everything that had happened impacted on her life.

She was extremely glad to see Catherine. She was the only person Paula would trust with the truth. She hoped she would help her make sense of it. They had a lot to catch up on.

'Doug was very impressed with you. He thought you were gorgeous. In fact, he spent the rest of the evening telling me how gorgeous you are.'

That surprised Paula. She had the impression that Doug had hardly registered her all evening. She suddenly realised that might well have been because he thought she was a call-girl. It would explain why he hadn't asked her about her job. Perhaps he hadn't forgotten to tell Ranji she was a friend and not a prostitute because he hadn't grasped the truth himself.

'Did he know who I was?' Paula asked.

'What do you mean?'

'I mean, did you tell him we were old friends?'

'Yes. Of course. What are you getting at?'

'Do you often go out on foursomes with his business associates?'

'Yes.' The expression on Catherine's face changed. 'Hold on. Let me guess. Ranji thought you were an escort, right? Oh Jesus, Doug is an idiot. I told him, Paula. I told him you were a friend. I spelt it out for him.'

'He obviously took it to mean "friend" in inverted commas.'

'What happened? Did Ranji hit on you?'

'Let's just say it was interesting. Is Doug in the habit of providing girls for his associates?'

'Sometimes. Some of them like a bit of company, especially if they're away from home. He relies on me. I've got this friend who runs an escort service. I organise a girl. We all go out to dinner together, then they peel off. But I told him a hundred times you were my friend. So what happened?'

They were sitting in a traffic jam waiting to go around Parliament Square.

'Quite a lot.' Paula couldn't help smiling. 'The whole evening was quite an experience for me.'

'Tell me, tell me.'

'Well . . .' Paula paused to look at her friend. She felt the same rush of lust for her she had on Tuesday. The skirt of her suit was short and her legs were sheathed in a shiny, champagne coloured nylon, the slender contours of her thighs changing subtly as she worked the pedals of the car. Her big bosom jutted out under the black jacket which was tightly buttoned to avoid the necessity of wearing a blouse. 'It was you and I that got me started. I mean, like I told you, I'd never experienced anything like that before. Never. I couldn't understand how my body could suddenly respond so intensely like that after years of being so . . . so . . . *impassive*. I was sure that the problem was that I'd been aiming at the wrong target all these years, and that perhaps what had made the difference was that, at last, I was with a woman.'

'I don't think that's true, Paula.'

'Please, let me finish. After what we got up to on Tuesday night, I was convinced. Completely convinced. I was absolutely sure I was a lesbian. I mean, you told me you'd always had huge pleasure with men and women. I'd only had it with women. Therefore, I thought, I'm a lesbian. I was sitting in that restaurant looking at all the women and wondering which ones I'd like to take to bed. I was on a real high. I'd never had sex like that and I wanted more.'

'And?'

'In the taxi Ranji asks me if Doug has taken care of everything. I haven't got the faintest idea what he means. Anyway he pays off the cab and takes me up to his suite without a by-your-leave.'

Catherine was laughing. 'Oh my God, what did he do then?'

'He gives me a drink then goes to the bedroom. Five seconds later he comes back naked apart from this tiny little towel.'

Catherine was laughing so much, little tears were forming in the corners of her eyes.

'And?'

Paula told her. She told her how she had not disillusioned Ranji, but had gone along with him, playing the whore. She told Catherine everything Ranji had done to her, and the fact that he was the best lover she'd ever had in her life. She also told her that she found it hard to understand what had happened to her since the night she'd lain supine on Catherine's bed with a sleeping mask over her eyes. She was, she told her finally, terribly confused.

'It's not so difficult to understand, is it?' Catherine asked when she'd finished. She'd managed to find a parking space in Beauchamp Place, a little way down from the new shop. It was festooned with bunting and balloons, and people milled about on the pavement, waiting to get inside.

'It's difficult for me,' Paula said earnestly.

'Look, you told me you weren't very good at sex, right? I gave you a practical demonstration to show you where you were going wrong. So let's say your body got the message. It's as simple as that.' Catherine shrugged.

'It's not simple at all. How can I get turned on by you, then find myself coming like it's going out of fashion with the first man I meet?'

'According to you he was the best lover you'd ever had and the most attractive. Isn't that what you said?'

'Yes,' Paula agreed.

'Paula, it's not black and white. I told you, I've always loved sex. Sex with women and men. They are not mutually exclusive, despite what dedicated homosexuals would have us believe. Sex with a woman is different that's all. You can enjoy both. And let's face it that's exactly what you've just done.'

Paula was grateful for her friend's common-sense. 'You really can have both?'

'Of course.' Catherine laughed. 'Sometimes at the same time! Come on, let's see what they've got. I'm in the mood to spend some of Doug's money. I'll let him think you were incredibly embarrassed by what happened with Ranji and I had to placate you with an Armani dress.'

'Sounds like a good idea!'

Catherine handed in an engraved invitation at the door and a girl in a fore-shortened white Roman toga with a gold belt and gold Roman sandals handed them both a glass of champagne. The shop was divided into two. On the ground floor was outerwear, dresses, suits and coats and an exclusive line of shoes. On the first floor it sold an equally exclusive line of lingerie; exotic creations in every material, from conventional silk, satin and lace to more *outré* items hidden away in a special room. Here Paula found herself browsing among garments made from incredibly thin and soft leather, suede and shiny rubber.

'I'm going to have to bring Doug here,' Catherine said.

'Is he into this?'

'Doug's into everything,' Catherine replied.

Catherine bought two lacy bodies and a tight waspie corset and encouraged Paula to try on a whole variety of underwear. Standing in the changing room, Paula paraded in front of a full-length mirror, her body transformed by tight crimson satin, or white lace, or shiny black lycra. She was astonished how lingerie completely changed her appearance, setting an agenda. She was provocative and challenging in dark coloured basques and underwired bodies, acquiescent and feminine in cream camisoles and French knickers. She elected to buy several of the items she had tried on.

Downstairs they each bought a slinky evening dress,

Catherine's tight with a halter neck in her favourite red; Paula's maroon and strapless with a knee-length skirt, made from a material that shimmered in the light. Paula also bought three pairs of high heels, shoes which as little as a week ago she would have dismissed as impractical and uncomfortable. Catherine insisted on paying for the dress and lingerie. She would present Doug with the bill and tell him it was the least he could do after what he'd put Paula through. The irony of this made them both laugh. Paula insisted on paying for the shoes herself, despite the fact that next week, she thought wistfully, she might find herself out of a job.

'Right,' Catherine said as they loaded their carrier bags into the car. 'Back home for a dress parade and something to eat?'

'Why not?' Paula said. She was glad of the opportunity to take her mind off Robert Parker, George Fairbrother and Alma Klein. Of course her relationship with Catherine had changed fundamentally now. They were no longer just friends. They were lovers. 'A dress parade and something to eat,' implied a whole different set of possibilities than would once have been the case, but Paula found she didn't mind that in the least.

They drove to Catherine's house in relative silence, the sort of silence that occurs naturally between old friends. Paula was glad of it. She wanted to think about what Catherine had said earlier. Catherine had a great deal more experience of sex than she had. She was prepared to accept her explanation. In fact, it was self-evidently true. She had conducted the experiment herself. The last thing she would have expected after having such intense sexual satisfaction with a woman, was an equally intense sexual experience with a man, but that is precisely what had occurred. One had fed off the other. The more she thought about it the more Paula began to see that, far from being mutually exclusive, the two experiences were like two pieces of a sexual jigsaw, slotting together perfectly to make a whole. Wasn't an element of what had happened with Ranji a desperate need to have a man deep inside her, after the non-penetrative sex with Catherine?

As they pulled into the drive of her house, Catherine operated a switch on a small black box on her dashboard and the garage door swung open. It descended again as soon as the car was inside. They gathered their bags together and Catherine de-activated the burglar alarm set on the garage wall by the interior door. They walked through into the house.

'Make yourself at home. I'll get us a bottle of champagne.'

'What a good idea.'

As Paula slumped into one of the large sofas in the sitting room Catherine took a bottle of Taittinger from her fridge. She didn't bother with an ice bucket, putting the bottle on a tray with two glasses.

'Here's to discoveries,' she said after she'd poured the wine.

Paula raised her glass and grinned. '*Self* discoveries.'

'I think it's snowing,' Catherine said.

Sure enough, outside the window large flakes of snow were floating down in the orangey glow of the street lights. The ground was dry and the snow settled immediately. In minutes everything had been coated in a layer of crisp white.

'Looks pretty. I always loved snow when I was a child,' Paula said.

'It makes everything go so quiet.'

They listened. The snow muffled the sound of the city outside.

'Come on,' Catherine said. 'Let's go and try on your new dress. You bring the bags, I'll take the champagne.'

Paula gathered up the shopping. She was intensely conscious of the fact that her heart was beating much faster than normal. In her whole life she had never been more aware of her breasts and her sex. She would swear that, since Monday night, her nipples had been permanently hard, two stone pebbles buried in her bra. Her sex, she was equally convinced, had been constantly moist. It didn't help that her clitoris and her labia were sore from the pounding Ranji had given them, his thick, wiry pubic hair rubbing against them like sandpaper. Whenever she moved the gusset of her panties rubbed against the tender flesh, reminding her physically of what he had done to her, and causing a stream of mental images to flow into her head. The images were not in chronological order. Catherine's naked body and open labia were juxtapositioned with Ranji's rampant erection plunging into her sex.

In her spacious bedroom, Catherine put the champagne and the glasses on one side of the bedside tables and stripped off the jacket of her suit. Her big breasts were confined in a black lace bra. Quite unselfconsciously, she unzipped her skirt and wriggled out of it. She was not wearing panties under her tights.

'I'm going to take a shower,' she said. 'Do you want to join me?' she added with a coquettish expression, one blonde eyebrow raised.

Paula stared at her. For once she was not surprised at the surge of desire that she felt, or its intensity. She was becoming accustomed to her new-found sexuality and the demands it made on her. It made her body hum.

Catherine disappeared into the bathroom leaving Paula to make up her own mind.

If the pace of events in Paula's life were hotting up, it was about time, she thought. For too many years she had stood on the sidelines watching life go by, sacrificing everything to the demands of her career. And where exactly had that got her? Her success at Lichtman Terry hadn't protected her from the threat of being fired, and there was little prospect, if she was, of ever being able to persuade another employer that George Fairbrother had acted unfairly.

The pace of the sexual revolution she had experienced in the last week had left her breathless. Any idea that she was physically incapable of enjoying the extremes of sexual pleasure, that she had a low sex drive and wasn't very good at sex, had been thrown out of the window. She had no intention of giving them house room again. Tonight, it would have been quite understandable if she had told herself that she should rest, that she should allow herself to get her breath back, and not have too much of a good thing. But that wasn't how she felt at all. She was on a rollercoaster ride and didn't have any intention or desire to get off.

She heard the shower running. Taking a sip from her glass of champagne she stripped off the cardigan, blouse and long skirt she had worn to work. Her white slip, cotton underwear and tights followed. Feeling a sense of exhilaration at her boldness she walked, naked, into the bathroom.

There was a glass shower stall in one corner, and she could see the outline of Catherine's body through a veil of steam. Catherine's bra and tights lay on the marble floor. A whole wall of the bathroom was lined with mirrors and Paula stared at her body. Her high breasts, narrow waist and flat belly bore no tell-tale signs of their recent adventures. She looked into her eyes but could see nothing there either to indicate the change that had overtaken her so rapidly.

'Hi,' Paula said as she opened the shower cubicle door.

'Come on in,' Catherine said. Her big breasts were

trembling under the cascade of water, her blonde hair plastered to her head.

Paula felt a second rush of desire but it was mixed with another strong emotion. She realised just how much she had always liked Catherine. Her determination to enjoy herself and her lack of ambition and consequent inattention to work, had annoyed Paula at university. But it was Catherine who had been responsible for showing Paula that sex did not have to be a pleasureless grind, and she was grateful. It wasn't just sex. It had come at a moment in her life when Paula realised that all work and no play was making her half a person, a pawn of the George Fairbrothers of this world, entirely dependent for her sense of well-being on work-orientated achievements.

'You look gorgeous,' she said eyeing her friend's naked body as the water flooded over it. The hair sticking to her head made Catherine look younger and less composed, the mask of cosmetic and coiffured elegance she presented to the world, washed away.

Paula stepped into the cubicle, closed the door behind her, and reached up to stroke Catherine's cheek. She leant forward and kissed her lightly on the mouth. Their breasts touched, the jets of water flowing over their bodies.

'Thank you,' Paula said seriously.

'For what?'

'Everything. I thought I'd be scared of all this. But I'm not. It's exciting. I love it.'

'Good.'

Catherine wrapped her arms around her friend and hugged her, their breasts crushing together. They kissed again, lightly at first, but then more hungrily, their mouths gnawing at each other, water eddying around their lips. They squirmed their bodies against each other, their pubic bones grinding from side to side. Paula felt a now familiar surge of pleasure that made her senses tingle, her body gearing itself up for more.

'You feel good,' she whispered into Catherine's ear.

'And you,' Catherine replied.

Paula knew what she wanted now. She pushed Catherine back against the glass wall of the cubicle and sank to her knees. Despite the water flooding off Catherine's belly she pushed her thighs apart and ran her tongue up into her puffy labia. As her tongue found her clit she snaked her left hand around the back of Catherine's thigh until her fingertips were pressing into the mouth of her vagina. She pushed her tongue up and down, dragging Catherine's clitoris with it. At the same time she tried to thrust her fingers into her vagina, but the water, perversely, had made it dry, washing away the natural lubricant, and sealing it. Paula pulled her fingers back not wanting to hurt her friend.

'It's all right,' Catherine hissed, 'just force it.'

Paula did exactly that. She wriggled her fingers against the dry, unyielding slit. It felt as though the edges had been glued together.

'Harder,' Catherine encouraged.

Paula pushed again. Catherine's labia were pressed upward but still did not give way. Paula wriggled a single finger between them and suddenly, like prying an oyster open, the seal parted and Paula's finger was plunged into Catherine's sex. It was an extraordinary sensation. The seal had worked both ways, keeping the water out, but also holding the sticky juice of her excitement in. Her vagina was soaking with a hot, viscous fluid.

'Oh yes,' Catherine cried the impact of the sudden thrust taking her by surprise.

'Feels like warm honey.'

Paula pushed two, then three fingers into Catherine's sex.

Having breached the dam there was no resistance. She felt the tube of Catherine's vagina spasm around the intruders. She could feel her clitoris throbbing too. She tried to ignore the water splashing into her face and synchronise the rhythm of her tongue to the inward stroke of her fingers, because she knew that was what she would want to feel if Catherine was doing this to her.

Catherine moaned loudly, opening her legs as wide as the confines of the cubicle would allow, so her labia were spread further apart and access to her clitoris was easier. Her sex seemed to suck at Paula's fingers, drawing them up into her body. Paula's assault had been so sudden and unexpected that she felt herself lurching towards orgasm in seconds. The water lashing down on her breasts was an extra provocation. She felt her muscles go rigid and, as quickly as that, she was coming. A delicious wave of pleasure coursed through her, her fingers digging into Paula's shoulders for support.

Slowly, as the tendrils of orgasm released her from their grip, Catherine slid down the glass until she was kneeling face to face with her friend. 'You're getting good at that,' she said.

'I want to be good at it. I want to be very good at it.'

They kissed again, their tongues weaving around each other like the mating dance of two snakes, one mouth hosting the event, then the other. Paula let her fingers slip out of Catherine's body. Almost immediately she felt Catherine's hand gliding over her back. She was holding an oval-shaped bar of soap. Gently she worked the soap between Paula's buttocks and down to her labia, creating a thick lather. Paula had been so focused on wanting to give Catherine a good time she had hardly registered her own body's feelings. Now they came in a rush. The creamy lather between her legs, sensuous and soft, produced a flood of sensation. She felt that odd clenching in her vagina that she had come to associate with a flood of her juices, her sex accomplished now in producing this phenomenon. Her clitoris pulsed strongly hoping to draw attention to itself. It succeeded. Catherine's other hand caressed Paula's belly then dropped down to her labia at the front. She found the swollen nub of nerves and flicked it, not at all gently, from side to side, making Paula gasp, and tear her mouth away from the kiss, unable to concentrate on both. Her clitoris had felt sore earlier but now her body seemed to be able to convert that discomfort into pure pleasure.

'You love it, don't you?' Catherine said. She inserted the edge of the soap into Paula's labia, then pressed its tip up into her vagina. The thick lather she had manufactured lubricated the opening and as she pushed it up the whole bar disappeared inside Paula's body.

Paula responded reflexively. Her sex contracted sharply pushing the soap out. Catherine thrust it back in again. The dual impact of expulsion, followed rapidly by impulsion, created a huge shock of feeling. Paula moaned loudly. Catherine had clearly done this before, and learned the technique. She did not hold the soap in. Instead she held her hand ready to catch it as it was expelled, then jammed it back up again. Her vagina's reaction was automatic, but produced a sensation like nothing Paula had felt before. The nerves of her sex sang with pleasure as they contracted to force the slick, slippery intruder away, followed by a sharp burst of exhilaration as the soap shot out. It was the exact opposite of what Ranji had done to her. Instead of being comprehensively filled, the pleasure came from emptying, from voiding her body of the soap. It wasn't just that, of course. As Catherine's right hand played hide-and-seek with the bar of soap her left was strumming Paula's clitoris relentlessly. In seconds Paula's body was quivering, her breasts trembling, the waves of pleasure oscillating into the frequency of orgasm like a radio receiver tuning into a signal. As the signal got stronger the oscillations increased, great crests of feeling followed by deep troughs, the gap between the two getting even shorter.

'I'm coming . . .' Paula cried, the water washing into her mouth as she opened it, making her gasp for breath, giving her the feeling she was drowning in sensation. Her body gave one final convulsion, and as her sex contracted and the soap shot out from her vagina one last time, she came, her orgasm as strong and rich as any she had so recently become accustomed to.

'God, Catherine . . .'

The warm water flowed over them. Paula's mascara had run and she had big panda eyes, her hair a mass of rat's tails. Catherine's make-up too was smeared and messy, her hair knotted and flat. They looked at each other and started to laugh. Glamorous they were not.

'How did you get my number?' Paula said when she heard Ranji's voice.

'From Doug.'

'I see.' And Doug, presumably had got it from Catherine.

'This is really embarrassing.'

'What is?' Paula asked.

'I mean, my behaviour was unforgivable. Quite unforgivable,' Ranji said. He appeared genuinely upset. 'What can I say in my own defence? I can't think of a single thing. But I had to ring you to apologise.'

'It was just a mistake.'

'Why didn't you say something?'

That, of course, was a good question. 'I was enjoying myself too much.'

'I was so ashamed. It's just . . . I want you to understand . . . sometimes it's simpler . . . when I'm away from home.'

'You don't have to explain to me,' Paula said.

'I want to. Will you let me buy you dinner tonight? Please, I would really like to see you again so I could apologise in person.'

And not just apologise, Paula hoped. 'No,' she said decisively. 'Come to my house. I'm not a very good cook but I can grill a steak and toss a salad. It would be much more comfortable.'

'I accept. I'll bring the wine. It's very kind of you to be so understanding.'

She gave him the address.

'What time?'

'Eight.'

'Fine. I'll be there. I really do appreciate this.'

The call had taken her by surprise. Ranji was the last person she'd expected to hear from. As far as he was concerned she was a call-girl hired especially for the occasion and she had said nothing to disabuse him of that fact. Obviously Catherine had kept her promise to give Doug Latimer a hard time for impugning her friend's honour and he, in turn, had rung Ranji.

But the surprise was a very pleasant one and Paula was delighted at the prospect of entertaining Ranji again, not only because she had never fancied any man so much in her life. It was Thursday and she had drawn a complete blank with trying to find a way to get to Alma Klein. She had called her New York office and left messages, none of which had been returned, which was frankly, what she'd expected. Spending the night with Ranji Patra would be a good way of keeping her mind off the fact that, barring a miracle, Friday might well be her last day at Lichtman Terry.

She looked out of her office window. The rooftops were encrusted with snow but a thaw was underway and water dripped into every gutter. On the street, the piles of snow that had been shovelled to one side were melting too, its whiteness already turned to sludgy brown by the city's pollution.

She picked up the phone on her desk and punched in Catherine's number.

'Hi,' she said as Catherine answered.

'Hi, I was just going to call you.'

'Really? I've just had a call from Ranji.'

'I know. He called Doug.'

'Oh, I thought it would be the other way round. I thought you'd balled out Doug and he'd called Ranji to ask him to apologise.'

'I did ball him out. But apparently Ranji had already called. He wanted your number so he could book you for another night!'

'But he knows the truth now?'

'Oh yes, I got Doug to call him back. Pity – you could have earned yourself five hundred quid *and* had a good time.'

'Five hundred! Is that the going rate?'

'For someone of your class and distinction.'

'Looks like I'll have to do it for nothing then.'

'Tell me more.'

'He's coming round tonight. So he can apologise to me in person.'

'Lucky you. Can I come too?'

'You've got quite enough on your plate haven't you?'

'There's never enough. Anyway, listen, are you doing

anything for dinner on Saturday? Doug wants to apologise to you in person too.'

'Another business associate who needs someone to warm his bed?'

'No. Just the three of us. Promise.'

'I'm not sure I'll be very good company,' Paula said ruefully.

'You've still not got anywhere with Klein, then?' Paula had explained her difficulties to Catherine over the meal they had shared last night.

'No.'

'You can drown your sorrows with us.'

'All right – if you don't mind doom and gloom,' Paula said.

'We'll pick you up at eight-thirty.'

'Great.'

'Wear that new dress.'

'Don't worry. I won't disgrace you.'

'Call me tomorrow when you've got some news.'

'About Ranji?'

'That too!'

As Paula put down the phone her secretary opened her office door without knocking.

'Your four o'clock is here,' she said.

'Thank you, Julie. Show him in will you?'

A small, bespectacled man of about fifty shuffled into the room. What was left of his hair was white and he had large, bulbous eyes. He gave the impression that he found the world an alarming place and that he was wary of every sudden movement or sound. He carried a brown, very battered, leather attaché case, holding it up against his chest.

'Mr Harmsworth, it's nice to meet you. Won't you sit down?'

Paula leant over her desk and shook Harmsworth's small hand. His handshake was limp.

'Thank you. I'm not sure I'm going to be of much help to you Miss Lindsey.'

'Nevertheless it was nice of you to take the time. I just thought we should explore a few options.'

'Of course.' He sat down on an upright chair in front of Paula's functional metal desk, placing the attaché case on his knees and clutching its outer edge as if it contained priceless information he dared not let out of his grasp.

'You understand we're acting for Mr Parker in the Winkworth take-over?'

'Yes.'

'As I know Mr Parker values your opinion I just wanted to sound you out on an idea I'm trying to run with.'

If anything, this produced a more defensive posture in Harmsworth's body language, curling him further back into his shell. Despite his appearance, Gregory Harmsworth was regarded by many as Robert Parker's right-hand man. He had been with him since Parker set up London Capital Conglomerates and it was reputed, though not confirmed, that his attaché case contained all the company's secrets.

'Go on,' he said.

'Mr Parker wants to mount a take-over of Winkworth's because of its large manufacturing capability in the field of static chips.'

'Yes.'

'The problem with that is the acquisition does not give Parker access to the US market. All Winkworth's plants are in Europe. At least seventy percent of the static chip component business is in the US. That's where growth could be exponential.'

'Miss Lindsey, we've looked at that. There isn't a single

plant in the US that could cope with the sort of product we're manufacturing. Winkworth's is the only option.'

'I accept that. But you still need a marketing arm in the US to shift the greatly expanded output. Are you aware of a company called AutoTech Marketing? Wouldn't they be an ideal way of reaching your US market?'

'Ideal. We've tried to do a deal with them. They want too big a cut.'

'Mr Harmsworth can you confirm that LCC owns Fahrenheit Fabrication?' Paula said.

'That is correct.'

'It is profitable?'

'Not especially.'

'Does it form part of Mr Parker's current plans?'

'In what way?' Harmsworth said, frowning.

'If he received an offer for it would he be likely to accept?'

'What sort of offer?'

'I can't flesh it out at the moment. But in principle?'

'In principle, probably. In principle he'd probably jump at it if you want the truth. Fahrenheit's always been a pain in the arse. Sorry, excuse my language.' Harmsworth looked shocked at himself.

'Thank you. That's most helpful.'

'Is that all?'

'Yes. Thank you again for sparing the time to see me.'

'Mr Parker's back tomorrow.' His voice was full of trepidation.

'I know,' Paula said, showing him out.

When he was gone she sat at her desk again, staring out of the window. Harmsworth had confirmed for her everything she had worked out for herself. She had developed the perfect plan to deliver Winkworth's from Alma Klein's clutches and provide Parker with the marketing he badly needed. It all fitted in place. The only trouble was that her time was running out.

# *Chapter Five*

He was wearing black. A black polo neck sweater under a black jacket and black slacks. It made his complexion look darker and the whites of his eyes whiter.

'Come in,' Paula said as she opened the front door. She'd contemplated greeting Ranji dressed in nothing but her newly acquired red, high-heeled shoes and a dab of perfume. She'd thought better of it though. She was wearing the high heels but they were blue to match the blue jersey strap dress she was wearing. It was a dress she had bought some time ago but never worn because, on reflection, she thought it looked too tarty. Strangely when she tried it on earlier it had not seemed tarty enough. Clearly her perceptions of herself, like everything else, had changed.

'Thank you,' he said handing her two bottles of *Chateau Palmer* claret. 'You mentioned steak, so I thought claret.'

'Perfect. Come through. Would you like champagne or something else?'

'Do you have bourbon?'

'Jack Daniels?' She went to the shelf in the sitting room where she kept the booze and poured him a bourbon, deciding she would have the same. 'Ice?'

'Please.'

She hadn't put out any ice so she took the ice tray from the fridge and bashed it noisily against the draining board.

Six or seven cubes escaped and she divided them between the two tumblers.

'Cheers,' she said handing him the glass.

'Cheers.'

'It's nice to see you again.' Paula had thought a lot about Ranji in the last three days. A lot. She thought about those dark brown eyes that seemed to look right through her and that sculpted, athletic body, but most of all she'd thought about his cock, its size, its adamantine hardness, and what it had done to her. Her reaction to seeing him was a physical one. Her whole body seemed to be tingling.

'I've prepared a little speech,' he said.

'Speech?' She looked puzzled. She gestured for him to sit down. He sat on one of the small sofas and she sat beside him.

'To apologise.'

'Please – I think it's me who should apologise really, don't you? I led you on.'

'But it was unforgivable of me to assume . . .'

'Forget it.'

Not until their conversation earlier in the day had it occurred to Paula to ask herself why a man as attractive as Ranji resorted to using call-girls, even if they were provided at someone else's expense. But since he'd tried to explain she was mildly curious. Only mildly. If she were honest she couldn't have actually cared less about what Ranji did or did not do, so long as sooner or later, he took her upstairs and fucked her as comprehensively and gloriously as he had in the small hours of Wednesday morning.

'You don't appear to think it strange that I involve myself with such women?' he asked.

'I wouldn't have thought it was necessary for you, that's all. You are a very attractive man.'

'I am usually more comfortable with women when I can define the terms of engagement.'

He had a way of looking at her that reduced Paula to jelly. His eyes were focused on her in an unwavering gaze that she could only interpret as one thing: lust. Perhaps they were only reflecting what she knew she was feeling.

'Why is that?' she asked trying to resist the temptation to throw herself at him.

'I had a very unhappy experience a year or two ago. Very unhappy. A woman I loved . . .' A dark shadow passed over his eyes. 'She let me down. Very painfully I'm afraid.'

Paula felt her heart lurch. She suddenly saw a vulnerability in Ranji that made him even more appealing.

'I didn't want to get involved again,' he said. He took a sip of the bourbon.

'You don't have to explain to me,' she said.

'I know. It's not very appetising though, is it? A man who uses prostitutes?'

'I really don't care, Ranji. Really. After all I was the one who did all the using. I was attracted to you. I am attracted to you. Pretending to be a hooker made it easy to skip a lot of the normal social conventions.'

'Social conventions?'

'Like, making small talk, letting a decent interval pass before I rip your clothes off and rape you, that sort of thing.'

'I see.' He smiled. He had very white, very regular teeth.

'Now you know the truth, I've got to sit here politely for hours haven't I? I can't just strip off like I did the other night and ravish you. You'd be shocked if I did that, wouldn't you?'

'Utterly shocked. Unless . . .'

'Unless?'

'Unless we came to an arrangement.'

'What sort of arrangement?'

He was still smiling. He took his wallet from the inside pocket of his jacket and extracted a small wad of fifty pound notes. 'Here. Now you're a call-girl again, bought and paid for. Now you're free to behave any way you wish.' He dropped the notes into her lap.

Paula laughed. 'Oh, it feels really wicked.'

'What exactly did you want to do?'

'Well.' Paula got to her feet, the money falling to the floor. Her heart was racing, delighted at the turn of events. She could act the whore again. What could be better? 'Taking you upstairs would be a good start.'

'Let's go then, time is money in your business, after all.'

'Exactly. Couldn't have put it better myself. I haven't got all night.' Thank God, she thought, that wasn't true. 'But perhaps you'd better take a look at what you get for your money, first.' She pushed the straps of the blue dress down over her shoulders. It was quite loose fitting, and once she had wriggled it over her jutting bosom, it fell to the floor. She had dressed deliberately, knowing this moment would come. She was naked apart from the black lace La Perla suspender belt and the sheer black stockings she had bought on her visit to Courtney's. The stockings had wide, jet black welts that the taut suspenders pulled into long chevrons on her creamy thighs. As she had never worn stockings the effect they had on her was a total surprise. They made her feel wild and wanton. But there was a physical effect too. The tightness of the nylon banding her thighs and the suspender belt around her waist seemed to emphasise the openness of her sex. It felt exposed and vulnerable and for some reason that made it ultra-sensitive. It looked incredibly sexy too, the black silk and nylon above and below, and the long thin suspenders that bisected her thighs seemed to frame it, drawing the eye to the centre of the picture where her naturally neat pubic hair pointed at the apex of her thighs.

She saw Ranji's eyes dancing over her thighs, his excitement obvious.

'Do I look like a whore?' she asked.

'Yes,' he replied breathlessly.

'I want to behave like one too,' she added. 'Follow me.'

As he got to his feet she saw an erection was already tenting the front of his trousers. She, by the same token, could feel her wetness leaking out of her sex.

The bolder she pretended to be, the bolder she became. She strode out into the hall and mounted the narrow staircase, knowing Ranji was right behind her and would, in all probability, be able to see the folds of her sex. The thought of his eyes staring up at her excited her more. She was so intensely aware of her own body she thought she could feel her labia rubbing against her clitoris as she moved.

In her bedroom she kicked off her shoes and lay on the bed. She'd already stripped the bedding away. She'd planned it all. Propping her head against the pillows she crossed her ankles and laid her hands on her breasts, squeezing them slightly so they ballooned out between her thumb and fingers. 'Your turn, I think,' she said, keeping to the script she'd rehearsed.

Without a word Ranji stripped off his clothes. Paula watched critically, prepared to believe her excited state on Tuesday night had caused her mind to embellish the details of what she'd seen. But apparently it had not. His body was just as perfect as she remembered it.

He was wearing small white briefs. His erection was already so large it peeked out above the top of them.

'Well,' she said. 'What does the gentleman want for his money?'

Ranji skimmed the briefs down his legs, his cock springing up against his belly. He came up to the side of the bed and leant over, kissing her lightly on the mouth. The kiss deepened. Paula felt his tongue pushing between her lips. She sucked on it as she felt his arms snaking under the neck and the back of her knees. Effortlessly, without breaking the kiss, he lifted her into his arms, cradling her like a baby. She felt an amazing wave of pleasure. She had always dreamt of being carried, though she had no idea why it excited her so much.

Gradually, he lowered her to the floor, but only for a moment. His two hands moved to her buttocks and hoisted her up by them, her body sliding against his. Instinctively Paula twisted her legs around his back making it easier for him to grip her, his hands sliding under her thighs. He lifted her up until her now open crotch was level with his belly, then slowly, so slowly it seemed to take forever, lowered her on to his cock. She felt his glans nudge its way into her labia and then, entirely of its own accord, plunge into her vagina. He let her down a little more and his cock began the journey up into her.

'Oh God, that feels so good,' she said clinging to his neck.

He still didn't hurry. Slowly, as his hand lowered her on to it, his cock reared up into her, higher and higher. She had the sensation of being filled again, impaled on his rod of flesh that might easily have been made of steel.

Even if she had wanted to resist she knew it was useless to do so. The way he had taken possession of her, with such infinite care, parting the flesh of her sex with the irresistible force of gravity, was like nothing she'd ever felt before. That was not saying much of course. There were so many things, she realised now, that she had not experienced, so much to learn. And she wanted to try it all.

Being held in his arms, clinging helplessly to his body, would probably have been provocation enough, but feeling this great piston slide into the cylinder of her body was simply too much. It was as though her whole weight was supported by his cock, his hands not appearing to hold her at all now. She was coming before his glans reached the top of her vagina. By the time it was pressing hard against the neck of her womb, and her clitoris was hard up against the base of his phallus, her sex was convulsing around him. She clung to his body, just as her sex clung to his cock, her arms and legs locked around him, her orgasm roaring through her.

He held her tightly for a moment without moving, letting the crescendo of feelings die away, then began to buck his hips, pulling his cock out of her, then plunging it back in. Supporting her weight seemed to be a matter of no concern to him. He wasn't even out of breath.

'So good,' she whispered.

'I know. You're so wet. So tight . . .'

'You'll make me come again.'

'Good.'

His cock pumped into her as easily and deeply as if she'd been lying on her back. It was an amazing sensation. With her legs wrapped around his back her clitoris was pressed against the bone hardness of his erection and each thrust hammered directly against it. Barely had Paula's first orgasm faded away when a second began to pluck at her nerves. The first had been rooted in the depths of her sex, spreading out in wallowing bands of pleasure. The second was clitoral, sharp and quick, almost painful in its intensity.

He felt it. He felt her body shudder, the legs scissored around him crushing his waist, her fingers clawing at his back.

It was only the beginning.

'Is that something you read in the Kama Sutra?' she asked.

'Oh yes, in India there's a copy in every hotel bedroom,' he said lying down on the bed again, and grinning. 'That was position number twenty-three, monkey-climb-tree.'

'Now it's my turn,' Paula said, wanting to take the initiative.

She scrambled on to all fours and stuck her buttocks out at him. The black welts of the stockings that banded her thighs made her bottom appear soft and very white in contrast. Ranji caressed it with his hands, running his fingers down between her legs so they brushed her labia. Then he knelt on the bed behind her and reached forward to cup her breasts and she felt his cock butting into the cleft of her buttocks. It felt hot. Very hot. Hot and wet. She couldn't suppress a moan.

His fingers teased her nipples, pinching them then circling them back into the flesh of her breasts, until she could feel them against her rib cage, her breasts flattened. He moved his hips so his cock dipped into her labia again. This time his penetration was instantaneous, riding all the way up into her, her copious juices lubricating his passage. He pulled back, until he was almost out of her altogether, then plunged forward for a second time. His hands moved over her hips, then down to her bottom. She felt them spreading her buttocks apart.

He didn't need to say anything. That was the funny thing. The level of sensual communication they had established between them was so acute that he didn't have to say a word. She knew immediately his cock slid out of her vagina what he was going to do. It caused a cold stab of fear to lance through her. But the fear was accompanied by a surge of excitement so fervent it took her breath away.

Paula struggled to maintain her control. She had never

been buggered before. Once, the idea would have scared her so much she would have run a mile from any man who'd even hinted at it. Now, though her mind was telling her it was one step too far, her body was pulsing wildly at the thought.

Ranji's hands still held her buttocks apart. He was looking at the neat, puckered hole of her anus. She felt his cock nudge against it.

Paula glanced over her shoulder at him. His eyes looked into hers, their expression intense.

'Is it all right?'

She could have said no. He wouldn't have minded. He could have taken her in a hundred other ways that would not involve the possibility of pain. But that wasn't the point. It wasn't a question of being rational and cautious. She had done that all her life. She had no intention of going back to that now. 'Yes,' she said, firmly. 'Do it.'

He pressed forward instantly. She had no idea what to expect. The ring of muscles that formed her sphincter tensed involuntarily, resisting the intruder. He pressed harder. His cock was greased with the juices from her body, and suddenly Paula felt herself open and he slipped inside her rear. The penetration was not deep, only up to the ridge at the bottom of his glans, but a wave of pain stabbed through her, making her gasp for breath. In less time than it took for a thought to form in her mind to register a protest, the pain had been translated into pleasure, equally hot, equally intense pleasure. She gasped for breath. The pleasure was scarlet. It had radiated through her whole body so quickly that her eyes had been closed by it and all she could see was a pulsating scarlet mist, like disco lights responding to the beat of the music.

Ranji pushed forward again. His cock drove deeper.

Paula's reaction was the same. The wave of pain was twisted into an almost unbelievable pleasure. He waited, taking his time, as though he understood the process. As the pleasure ran its course, he thrust forward again, this time using the whole length of his cock, burying it so deeply in her that his heavy balls bumped against her labia. This time the pain was not so sharp, her body quickly inured to the intrusion. Again it turned to pleasure, but that was different too, mutating instantly from singular, stabbing ferocity to the sort of pulsing sensation that instantly sent signals to her clit. In seconds she felt a third orgasm overtaking her, leap-frogging through her nerves. His phallus completely filled her rear, stretching its length and its breadth but she found herself wriggling back on it as if wanting more.

She reached back with one hand, found the opening of her vagina with her finger and stuck a finger up into it. She could feel his cock sheathed by the membranes of her body. She heard her voice. It seemed to be a long way away. It was moaning, trying to force out a cry, without success. Her orgasm swallowed her up, her body shuddering, the edge of pain inexplicably making it more frenzied.

He held her firmly by the hips. She was shuddering. Eventually the tremors were stilled. Gently, he pulled out of her, causing a wave of sensation almost as powerful as what had gone before. He waited for it to die away.

'That was the first time for you, wasn't it?'

'Yes. Don't you want to come like that?'

'No.'

'What then?'

Even after the shattering orgasms she had experienced Paula was still on a high. She wanted more. She wanted his spunk. She needed it. She wouldn't feel complete without it. There was a time when sex meant little to Paula. At worse it had been a chore, at best an obligation. Her body had responded occasionally with a dull, muted and almost resentful climax, if it had bothered to respond at all. It had been a reflection of her own attitude. Sex was low on her agenda, if it was on her agenda at all.

In a week all that had changed. Fundamentally. She had simply had no idea that sex could be like this. She had never known what it was like to need a man like she needed Ranji. At that moment if someone had asked her to choose between becoming chief executive of Lichtman Terry and feeling Ranji come inside her, there would have been no contest. She had never wanted to feel anything more in her life. She knew it would make her come again and that her orgasm would surpass anything she'd felt so far tonight. But that wasn't the point. Passion and desire was. It was not her satisfaction that mattered, but his. She wanted him to come so desperately, because that was what sex was about. His wanting her, his need for her, his passion for her was what, ultimately, turned her on. She had never felt that before, never felt the passion of need, never felt that a man truly wanted her. That was what had been missing.

'This.'

With no gentleness at all, he took hold of her hips, pulling her back on to him as he rammed his cock into her vagina. It was burning hot, the control he had exercised thus far serving to inflame it. In her mind's eye, Paula could see it pushing into the silky soft walls of her vagina, and riding up into her. She was sure she could feel every vein in it pulsing and pumping, his spunk making him larger and harder, ready to burst.

'I'm going to come,' he hissed.

'Oh yes, yes. I need it.'

She knew she was coming too. It was unavoidable.

Irresistible. As she felt his cock kicking against the tight confines of the tube of her sex, her body clenched, her sex spasming. She could feel every inch of him in her vagina, but at the same time she could feel the shadow of his cock in her anus, nerves never touched before sparking into life as her orgasm exploded. In the middle of it all, in the centre of the vortex of pleasure that overwhelmed every part of her, she felt his cock twitching inside her. Whether it was true, or whether she just imagined it, she thought she could feel each separate jet of spunk as it sprayed against the walls of her vagina, in a seemingly endless stream, each accompanied by a violent recoil in his phallus. If it were possible, the sensation would have provoked a new wave of feeling, but it was not. Her body was not capable of any new response. It was sated, exhausted and, finally, replete.

She found herself day-dreaming. That was a new phenomenon in her life too. Her powers of concentration had always been limitless but in the last week she had found herself staring out of her office window at the black windows of the building opposite, lost in reverie.

She had good reason for it, Paula thought. Everything that had happened to her had happened so fast. She had had no time to digest it all, to cut it up into small pieces and compartmentalise it away, as she had always done with everything else. The trouble was, the experiences of the last two weeks weren't going to fit easily into any compartment, and so far refused to be tucked neatly away. They were too affecting.

Basically, she thought she was beginning to understand what had happened to her. For years she had been sublimating her sexual energy, throwing herself into her career. But energy can neither be created nor destroyed and her sexual energy had finally asserted itself, breaking free of the shackles she had imposed on it. The genie had escaped from the bottle and was eager to make up for lost time.

Eager wasn't the right word. Desperate would be nearer the mark. Last night, after she had fed Ranji on steak and salad and drunk both bottles of the claret, he had taken her again on the sitting room floor, their need, despite their early couplings, too urgent to wait until they could get upstairs. That might have been partly her fault of course, since she'd insisted on preparing dinner in just her suspender belt, stockings and high heels, and had only donned the black, lacy and near transparent silk slip while they ate. Her thirst for sex had, it seemed, become unquenchable.

It was also a delicious, vicious circle. The more she wanted sex, and the more she had dreamt of Ranji and what he had done to her, the greater the impact of his actual physical presence had been, making her orgasms sharper and more intense. The more intense her orgasms, the more she wanted him again and dreamt of what they had done. A perfect circle that amazed and delighted.

She was even more amazed at her reaction to Catherine. She had often had fantasies about men, despite her sexual ineptitude, but she had never once thought of a woman as a sexual object. She couldn't even remember looking at a woman with anything that vaguely approached sexual interest, so her response, and the ease with which she had fallen into lesbian sex, was a total surprise. Though she had been perfectly prepared to believe that it was an orientation she had suppressed – unconsciously for so many years, Paula was greatly relieved that Ranji had come along so quickly to dispel that illusion. In fact, now, she had gone from believing that she was a confirmed and dedicated lesbian only able to enjoy sexual ecstasy with a woman to the much more comforting thought that she was probably not homosexual at all and that her response to Catherine had been more to do with her gratitude and love for her oldest friend. She couldn't imagine going to bed with another woman, a stranger. Or could she? As it was prone to do recently her body shuddered involuntarily. That was a poser for another day.

The phone on her desk rang, startling her.

'Yes?'

'Will you come up? Now.' It was Fairbrother's voice.

'Certainly.'

Paula had been expecting his call. It was four-thirty. At four o'clock she had given up hope of reaching Alma Klein. She had spoken to a friend at a merchant bank that Klein used frequently and the woman had promised to see what she could come up with, but hadn't called back. If she could not pitch her strategy to Klein first, there was absolutely no point taking it to Robert Parker. Which meant that she had drawn a blank. Unless Fairbrother had undergone some sort of religious experience, he was going to use this as a perfect opportunity to get rid of a female executive whose appointment he'd tried to oppose in the first place.

Upstairs, Jean, Fairbrother's secretary, looked as if she were sitting outside the condemned cell. 'You're to go right in,' she said smiling sympathetically.

'It's all right,' Paula said. 'I've been expecting it.'

She knocked on Fairbrother's door and walked in without waiting for his response. George Fairbrother sat behind his desk. He was busy stuffing his mouth with chocolate digestive biscuits and some of the chocolate had melted on to his chin.

'Sit,' he said with his mouth full. He sipped a cup of tea noisily. 'Perhaps you'd like to explain to me why you had the bare-faced cheek to summon Gregory Harmsworth to your office without my permission?'

Paula sat down and crossed her legs. She was wearing her new black high heels and a pair of very sheer, gun-metal grey tights. For a moment, she found herself admiring the way they made her legs look, smooth and slender.

'I wasn't aware I needed permission.'

'Harmsworth's time is valuable.'

'I needed to speak to him. As Robert Parker was away he seemed the best—'

'About what?' Fairbrother interrupted.

'I believed I had a strategy that would solve the whole dilemma in relation to Winkworth's.'

'There is only a dilemma, as you put it, because of your incompetence. I'm sure it will not come as any surprise to you to learn that Parker has been in with Aaron Lichtman this morning. Nor that he is furious as to the unprecedented rise in Winkworth's share price, and equally annoyed that his most senior executive's time was wasted by one of this firm's more junior members.'

There was no point in defending herself but it was like a conditioned reflex. 'He was in the building anyway. He didn't come over especially to see me. I don't suppose I spent more than five minutes with him.'

'Five minutes too long. How can I put this, Ms Lindsey? You're fired.'

'You can't fire me.'

'I just have.'

'On what grounds?'

'On the grounds of your gross incompetence in relation to the acquisition of Winkworth's shares.'

Paula looked at him calmly. She had rehearsed what she was going to say. 'I shall go to a tribunal. I told you that I was not responsible for the rise in the share price. That is due to Alma Klein's interest in the company. When she launches a full bid you will see that and it will be clear I have been unfairly dismissed.'

'Please leave now.'

'I have been trying to put a package together that could earn this company a considerable fortune in commissions and fees. The fact that you have fired me will not stop me. I'll take my proposition direct to Robert Parker.' It was bluff of course. Unless she could get to Alma Klein she would have nothing.

'You will do no such thing.'

'Mr Fairbrother, you have just fired me. You are in no position to be able to determine my future actions.' Paula got to her feet. 'No doubt I'll see you in court.'

Paula sat in front of her dressing table on Saturday evening, putting the finishing touches to her make-up, curling mascara on to her long eyelashes. She had used more make-up than usual, darkening her eyes and hollowing her cheeks with blusher. She'd even varnished her finger and toenails, something she had done so rarely before that she had to go out and buy the varnish. She'd bought two new dresses, some more lingerie and hosiery and another pair of shoes too. Considering her financial future it was an extravagance, but she viewed it as a gesture of defiance against the world in general, and George Fairbrother in particular.

As well as changing her make-up, she had tried wearing her hair up. The strapless neckline of the maroon dress Catherine had bought her suited this style, emphasising her long, slender neck about the billowing curves of her bosom, straining out from the tight bodice.

She had chosen her lingerie carefully too. It was one of the first lessons she thought she had learned from Catherine. Looking good meant feeling good. The new dress and the equally new lingerie she had bought made her *feel* good. She had also discovered that the silky, tight, underwear was also a sensual pleasure in itself.

It wasn't only that of course. Presumably, as there was only the three of them going to dinner, she would be dropped back to her front door at the end of the evening. But she supposed it was possible that Doug Latimer might hurry off somewhere and leave her and Catherine alone, though she realised that was almost certainly wishful thinking.

She saw the Rolls Royce arrive and double park on the street outside. She had her small black evening bag ready. Without waiting for Catherine to come and get her, she set her house alarm and double-locked the front door.

Doug Latimer climbed out of the back seat and kissed Paula on both cheeks. He was wearing a tailored grey suit, a white shirt and a yellow Dunhill tie. 'You sit in the back with Catherine,' he said, as the chauffeur opened the rear passenger door.

Catherine looked devastating in a black chiffon tunic over a black satin body, its material embossed with diamanté across the box neckline. Her skirt was black chiffon too, layer upon layer of it, flounced and ankle length.

'You look gorgeous,' Paula said as she sat beside her on the leather seat.

'And you. What have you done with your make-up?'

'Just experimenting.'

The chauffeur got behind the wheel again. As the car pulled away, Doug wound down the glass partition between the front and rear seats and twisted round to talk to them.

'Look,' he said earnestly, 'I really owe you an apology about the other night.'

'No, you don't,' Paula said. 'I had fun.'

Doug raised an eyebrow. That wasn't the response he'd been expecting.

'I've been dealing with Ranji for years. He's more a friend than a business associate.'

'He's a lovely man,' Paula said. 'Really, you've got nothing to apologise for. In fact, I was flattered someone would be prepared to pay five hundred pounds to take me to bed.'

'Anyway this is my way of saying sorry.'

'And this,' Catherine said, indicating Paula's dress. 'Do you like it?'

Doug's eyes roamed Paula's body. They dwelt on the firm curves of her cleavage and spent an equally long time on her legs, as if trying to see up under the knee length skirt. He did it for a little too long.

'You can put your eyes back in their sockets now, darling,' Catherine said.

'Sorry,' he said, 'Force of habit.'

Paula didn't understand what that meant but let it pass.

The Rolls drew up outside the Connaught, two commissionaires hurrying to open both rearside passenger doors. Doug led the way into the Grill Room at the back of the hotel, and in the small intimate room, its *trompe l'oeil* imitating a country garden, they ordered a sumptuous meal. Doug had a long conversation with the *sommelier* who subsequently produced a *Chassagne Montrachet*, with the *Soufflé de Sole et Crabbe* and an *Haut Brion* to accompany the rack of lamb. *Chateau Y'Quem*, its colour like liquid gold, came with dessert.

Before, at their dinner with Ranji, Doug had been distant with Paula, perhaps because he had provided her – or so he thought – to entertain his client. Tonight, however, he talked to her as if they were old friends, telling her stories of his investment bank and generally being perfectly charming. They did have a lot in common. The world of finance and the City was a small one and most of the people he mentioned she knew.

She had decided not to mention the termination of her employment with Lichtman Terry. She'd told Catherine over the phone on Friday night and that was that as far as she was concerned. Tonight, she was being bought dinner at one of the most expensive restaurants in London and she was determined to enjoy it. She could prove to herself she was as capable as anyone else of fiddling while Rome burned.

That did not mean to say, since Doug was being so expansive, that it would do any harm to bring up one aspect of her current difficulties. As they chose desserts from a large, three-tiered trolley she launched into the subject.

'I don't suppose you've had any dealings with Alma Klein?' The waiter placed a glazed mango tart in front of her, the mango sliced as thinly as razor blades and fanned out in a circle.

'The American? She's a bitch.' For the first time Paula was aware of a slight slur in his voice. He had ordered two bottles of claret and had consumed most of one of them himself.

'But you know her?'

'Sure. She's good. She's very good. I swear she's had a pair of balls sewn on.'

'I need to get hold of her.'

'Why?'

'I think I've identified an area of mutual interest with a client of mine.' She did not bother to explain that Parker was now officially an 'ex' client.

'And?'

'Could you introduce me?'

'No problem. You'll have to be extra nice to me, of course.'

'Of course.'

'Tomorrow,' Doug said.

'What do you mean?'

'Do you want to meet her tomorrow?'

'She's in New York.'

'No, she's not. She's in London. I talked to her yesterday as a matter of fact. She's a partner in a joint venture I've got going. Funnily enough it's to finance the development of Ranji's fuel cell.'

'She's here?' Paula could hardly believe it. It made sense though. If she was going to launch a bid for Winkworth's, she would need to talk to their institutional share-holders in London.

'She always stays at the Dorchester. It'll have to be tomorrow though, she's going back to New York on Monday.'

'Could you call her for me?'

'Consider it done.'

Paula ate her sweet. If she could get in to see her tomorrow and Alma Klein liked what she had to say, Monday might not be her first day of unemployment after all.

'Coffee, sir?' the waiter asked as he cleared away the desserts.

'Let's have coffee at home, shall we?' Doug said.

Catherine's hand touched Doug's arm. 'Doug . . .' she said with a clear admonition in her voice.

'Paula doesn't mind,' he said.

'No, that's fine with me. As long as your car takes me home afterwards.'

'Naturally.' He dismissed the waiter with a nod of his head.

'Doug, you know Paula's just a friend,' Catherine said.

# THE WAYS OF A WOMAN

'Of course I know. That's why we're here, isn't it? To apologise for mistaking her for one of your other friends. One of your naughty friends. She's got some very naughty friends, haven't you, Cath?' He had finished the last of the *Y'Quem* and was clearly the worse for wear.

'I think we'd better go.'

'Yes, let's do that.' He made a hand signal for the bill. The head waiter nodded and disappeared behind the glass topped oak panelled partition in one corner of the room. In a moment he was back with a bill on a small silver tray which Doug signed without reading and immediately got to his feet, swaying slightly.

'I think we should take Paula home now,' Catherine said in a very firm tone.

'Paula can make up her own mind, darling. She's a big girl.'

The Rolls was waiting outside. Catherine gave Doug a venomous look. The two women climbed into the back seat but instead of getting in the front, Doug pushed in between them.

'This is cosy,' he said, grinning.

'It was a beautiful meal, thank you,' Paula said.

Doug gripped her knee. 'You are going to come in for coffee, aren't you?'

She saw Catherine looking at her, suggesting by shaking her head that she should refuse. But she didn't want to antagonise Doug, not with the prospect of an introduction to Alma Klein very much on the cards. 'If that's what you want,' she said.

'Good.' He looked at Catherine. 'You see,' he said meaningfully as if he'd won a significant point in some private argument.

The car parked outside Catherine's house. The chauffeur

ran around to open the back door. Catherine got out first followed by Doug, who strode up to the front door of the house and opened it with his own key, murmuring something about having to pee.

'What's the matter?' Paula said as she got out of the car, and they walked into the house at a more leisurely pace.

'Just be careful,' Catherine said. 'I know what happens when he gets into one of those moods.'

'What?'

'He wants to sleep with you, Paula. With both of us.'

Catherine closed the front door behind them. They could see the light on in the cloakroom to the right. Doug hadn't closed the door properly and they could hear a continuous splashing sound.

'With both of us!' Paula might have expected her reaction to be one of horror. Instead she felt only excitement.

'Occasionally he likes me to get one of the escorts . . . he pays them to sleep with us.'

'The three of you?'

'He's just trying it on with you.'

Doug came out of the cloakroom, drying his hands. 'I need a brandy,' he said.

'You've had quite enough haven't you?' Catherine said.

'You are in a bad mood tonight. What's the matter with you?' He slipped his arm around Catherine's waist and hugged her. She did not attempt to shrug him off. They walked into the living room together.

Paula's mind was racing. If Catherine and Doug slept with an escort girl, did that mean the girl was expected to service both of them? She knew it was a common fantasy for a man to want to watch two women making love. Was that why Doug wanted to do it? Did he get turned on by seeing Catherine with another woman? That thought provoked a pang of emotion Paula did not recognise at first. Then she realised it was jealousy at the thought of Catherine with some other woman. But that was absurd. She certainly felt no jealousy at the thought of her with a man.

Doug poured three large measures of brandy into three brandy balloons, without asking Paula or Catherine if that's what they wanted. Catherine walked through into the kitchen and put the coffee machine on.

'Here,' Doug said handing Paula a glass then slumping on to one of the sofas.

'I think I've had enough,' Paula said, taking the glass nevertheless. She sat in a small armchair by the fireplace. She found herself considering what it would be like to go to bed with him. She looked at his face and his body. He was not as fit and athletic as Ranji but he was a handsome man. His eyes radiated an intensity, an appetite for life, that was extremely attractive.

'You're a gorgeous woman,' he said. He took a gulp of the brandy.

'Thank you,' Paula said. He was looking at her but his eyes weren't focused. She wondered if he knew she had been to bed with Catherine and was trying to imagine the scene.

'I'd like to kiss you,' he said focusing again.

'Wouldn't Catherine object?' Paula said trying to pretend innocence.

'Catherine,' he shouted through to the kitchen. 'Do you object if I kiss Paula?'

Catherine stormed back into the room. 'Yes, I bloody well do,' she said angrily, standing in front of him with her hands on her hips. 'I told you, Doug, she's not available. I thought you understood that.'

'I did,' he said quietly. 'But there's no harm in asking, is there? I mean, I'm going to do her a big favour tomorrow.'

He laughed. 'I thought she might like to show her gratitude.'

'That's typical of you. Never do something for nothing.'

'That's business,' he said.

'She doesn't have to put out because of that,' Catherine said. 'You'll make the introduction anyway, won't you?' Her tone was still angry.

'Of course, of course, just joking. I just thought, since the three of us were together . . .'

'Forget it.'

Paula sipped her brandy. She felt breathless. Her pulse was racing and felt hot. 'Isn't anyone going to ask what I want?' she said.

'I'll get the car to take you home,' Doug said.

'I don't want to go home.' Paula got to her feet. Everything that had happened to her over the last week had changed the way she felt about her sexuality. But it had also had another effect. It had made her more assertive, brasher and more daring. With studied deliberation, she ran her hand over Catherine's upper arm, the chiffon sleeve rasping slightly against her palm, then leant forward and kissed Catherine on the lips very lightly, just brushing her mouth and the tip of her tongue against them. 'This is what I want,' she said decisively.

# Chapter Six

Paula felt Catherine's body shiver. She kissed her harder, running her arm around her back and pressing their bodies together. She felt Catherine's breasts crushing into hers. She could feel her nipples too, small but already hard.

'You don't have to do this,' Catherine said as she stepped back.

'I know. I want to.'

Her body was tingling with pure sexual excitement. It reminded her of what she had felt when she'd taken Catherine up to her bedroom, or when Ranji had scooped her into his arms. The prospect of going to bed with Catherine and Doug was thrilling. She wasn't sure which excited her most, the thought of being with Catherine again, or of having a new man. But it didn't matter. She could have her cake and eat it too, the softness of a woman followed by the hardness of a man, the perfect answer to the dichotomy of her sexual feelings.

'Quite a girl isn't she, honey?' Doug said. His eyes were locked on Paula. 'Do I take it you two are more than just good friends?'

'See for yourself,' Paula said. She took Catherine's cheeks in both her hands and kissed her full on the mouth, pushing her tongue out and squirming her lips against her friend. The kiss aroused her, as it had done before, the planes and angles of a woman's body still a surprise to her. But the arousal was increased by Doug's presence, by the fact that she knew his eyes were watching them avidly.

The kiss was a statement. It told Catherine, she hoped more than words could do, that this was a situation she found intensely exciting. And Catherine got the message. Her body changed, its stiffness melting away. Without another word, Paula took her hand and led her upstairs. They heard Doug following behind them but did not look back.

The bedroom was warm, the curtains already drawn. Catherine put on one of the bedside lamps and dimmed it until the room was bathed in a pleasant glow. She came up behind Paula and unzipped the maroon dress, then turned so Paula could do the same to her skirt. Doug kicked off his shoes and sat on the bed, pulling his socks off.

It was going to be as easy as that, Paula thought. What was that French expression? *Ménage à trois*. In a matter of a few minutes, all the normal social barriers had been dropped, the inhibitions built up over years, abandoned casually. There was a time when Paula would have thought of this situation as perverted and morally reprehensible. Now it served only to create a need so strong it became the focus of everything she was, allowing room for nothing else.

Catherine caught her eye. She smiled a smile of reassurance. It said she hoped this would not change anything between them. Her eyes had not lost their look of worry and concern and she was clearly not convinced her friend was doing the right thing. She dropped the black chiffon skirt to the floor and stepped out of it, then draped it over a chair. She pulled the tunic off and sat on the bed in the tight black satin body. Doug had taken his jacket and tie off downstairs. Catherine began unbuttoning his shirt.

Paula was the centre of attention. She wriggled the dress

over her bosom and down her waist. Despite the zip being undone, the material clung to her body. It was not until Paula had wrestled it to her knees that it finally fell to the floor.

At the shop opening Catherine had taken her to, Paula had bought a basque. It was made from a modern fabric that hugged and clinched her body in an unyielding grip whilst being almost transparent. The white garment had a low cut bra edged in white satin and long satin suspenders supporting white, lace-topped stockings. The stockings were long and the welts almost brushed against Paula's labia. She wasn't wearing panties.

Doug began to laugh. 'Is this a wind-up? Have you two cooked this up between you. Jesus, she looks good enough to eat.'

'You look gorgeous, Paula, beautiful,' Catherine said quietly.

Doug stripped off his shirt. He had a broad and hairless chest, but though he was not fat he had none of the muscle definition Ranji displayed.

Catherine got to her feet. She bent to undo the three poppers in the gusset of the black body then drew it up over her head. She was wearing a black bra to support her breasts and matching black panties under her tights. She reached behind her back to unclip her bra. Her breasts fell free.

'Looking at her's made me hard,' Doug said to Catherine.

'Show me,' Paula said boldly, staring into his lap.

Doug stood up. The bulge of his erection stuck out under his trousers.

'He's a big boy,' Catherine said. The desire she felt for Paula had washed away her reservations. Her friend was an adult, after all, and capable of making her own decisions. No one was forcing her. She walked up behind Doug and pressed her naked breasts into his shoulder blades, as she ran her hands down to the belt of his trousers. She unbuckled it and unzipped his fly, then reached inside and extracted his cock. It was already nearly fully erect, the glans still partly covered by his foreskin. Wrapping her fist around it Catherine jerked his foreskin back so forcefully it made him moan.

'Lovely,' Paula said. Obeying the dictates of instincts she had so recently developed, she dropped to her knees in front of Doug, pulled his trousers down to his knees and slipped her mouth over his cock. Instantly she felt her sex throb almost as though it had been penetrated, the empathy between it and her mouth total. She gasped, expelling a rush of hot air against the phallus.

Catherine pulled off her tights. The tiny black panties were no more than two small triangles of silk clinging to her pubis and stretched tightly over her bottom but she kept them on. Kneeling behind her friend, her legs apart and spread on either side of Paula's she pressed her body into Paula's back. She ground her heavy breasts into Paula's shoulders as she reached around to cup her breasts.

Paula bobbed her head back and forth on Doug's erection. It was big. It was hard, too, and hot. She took it as deep as she could, pushing it right down into her throat then pulling it almost all the way out and sucking it strongly.

'What a pretty sight,' Doug said as Catherine's hands smoothed over the white basque, plucking at her nipples through the material of the bra cups. Her left hand then strayed lower, over the front of the tight garment, then down on to Paula's pubes. She thrust a single finger up between her labia. Doug felt the effect. Paula gasped again but did not lose the rhythm she'd established.

Catherine's finger stroked up and down. With all the unaccustomed attention it had had in the last week Paula's clitoris seemed to have become permanently enlarged. She had never felt it so big. Nor so tender. All the activity had made it sore, but that discomfort was wiped away by a flood of feelings as Catherine's finger caressed it. Catherine seemed to know exactly what to do, the right tempo, the right pressure, the right spot. It was delicious. It was better than that. The cock in her mouth and Catherine's finger seemed to be linked, magically, together. The enormous charge she got from one was more than doubled by the presence of the other.

That was the cause of her physical arousal, but there was a psychological dimension too that increased her exhilaration. Not only was all this completely new to Paula, it had an element of the forbidden, of being taboo. Social shibboleths had been suspended. Paula had never done anything like this before, never even watched a blue movie, and here she was, quite suddenly, in what could easily have passed for one.

Catherine's hand slipped from Paula's breast. It caressed her back, then curled over her buttocks and down between her legs until the tips of her fingers were nosing into Paula's vagina. Two fingers, then three penetrated her, screwing up into her until the knuckles of her hand prevented further progress, while Catherine pressed her mouth against Paula's neck and began sucking and licking at it.

Paula shuddered. She tried to say something, but the words were gagged on Doug's cock.

Doug pulled away. Paula didn't want that, but she was powerless to prevent it. Her body had been pitched into a storm of feeling. She was coming already, her orgasm mounting with the perfectly timed rhythm of Catherine's finger stroking against her clit which, in turn, was matched to the fingers sliding up and down in her vagina. Paula arched her head back over her shoulder in the hope of reaching Catherine's mouth. They kissed awkwardly, their mouths askew, their tongues dancing around each other, their saliva hot and sticky. She could feel Catherine's nipples on her shoulder blades. She wanted to touch them, she wanted to turn and press their breasts together, she wanted to kiss her and look her in the eyes, but there was no time. Her orgasm was approaching like an express train. All she could do was look up at Doug, look into his eyes, and display herself for him, let him see what no man had ever seen, her body being pleasured by another woman.

'Oh Cath, Cath . . .' she screamed, as Catherine's fingers twisted into her sex and she felt the surge of orgasm leap from her clitoris, arcing into her vagina, then out over the rest of her body. The tight constriction of the corset seemed to hold it in, imprisoning it so it could not escape, making it more intense and long lasting. Or was that just her fevered imagination?

'Very pretty,' Doug said. He pulled off his trousers and briefs and sat on the bed.

Paula felt Catherine's fingers slip gently from her body. On impulse she turned round and grabbed her wrist, bringing her hand up to her mouth, then sucking on her fingers. She was behaving like a slut, but it was so exciting. She tasted her own juices, and smelt the musky aroma of sex. She realised she was capable of anything. That realisation energised her. Even during the course of the last week she had never felt like this, so exhilarated and so alive.

Getting to her feet Paula helped Catherine up too. 'Lie on the bed,' she said, asserting herself once again.

'What are you going to do?' Catherine asked, in a tone of voice that suggested wide-eyed innocence.

'Don't take her panties off,' Doug said.

'He likes to pull them aside,' Catherine explained. 'One of his many little quirks.' She lay on her back on the bed.

Paula knelt up on the mattress beside her. Immediately she forced Catherine's legs open with her hands and dipped her head down between them. Her tongue licked the black satin that covered Catherine's labia, then pressed the material up into her vagina, before using her fingers to pull the crotch of the panties to one side. She eased her tongue into the very top of her labia. It found its target. Catherine's clit was engorged. She moaned as Paula tapped it with the tip of her tongue, then began circling it.

Out of the corner of her eye Paula saw Doug watching them, his cock sticking up vertically from his lap. She had never imagined that being watched like this would be exciting but she found that the look in Doug's eyes, the desire and lust, excited her very much.

Doug knelt on the bed, just as she was doing. He 'walked' forward on his knees until his cock was poised above Catherine's mouth. Digging a hand into one of her generous breasts, his fingers creating deep channels in the flesh, he sawed his cock to and fro across her lips, then pushed himself downward so she could swallow it.

Paula felt her sex throb. She burrowed one hand under Catherine's thigh and pushed her fingers up into her vagina. The walls of her vagina were wet and silky. Having sex with a woman was such a new experience for her that every element of it still took her by surprise, creating surges of pleasure. As she pumped her fingers in and out of Catherine's sex, the feeling of it, the way the folds of it parted to admit her, then closed again as she pulled back, thrilled her anew. It was as if she were touching her own body, that was the peculiar thing. She could feel in her own sex everything Catherine was feeling. It was the same with Catherine's clitoris. She could actually feel it pulsing against her tongue, but hers was pulsing just as strongly and with exactly the same tempo.

With such an intimate connection, it was not difficult for her to sense the subtle changes in Catherine's body as the dual assault stirred the tendrils of orgasm. The softness of a woman's mouth and the hardness of a man's cock. They were the perfect combination Paula realised. She had rushed into this experience, motivated by blind lust, but if she had thought – somewhere at the back of her mind – that it was a mistake which she would live to regret, she was certain, now, that it was not. Her instincts had been right. It was a glorification of her body's new-found ability to respond sexually, a testament to her daring, and a statement of her sexuality. Like a butterfly emerging from a chrysalis, she felt as if her wings were unfolding, as if she could quite literally fly. She was the perfect imago.

Catherine's body arched up off the bed. Her sex contracted tightly around Paula's fingers. She moaned, the sound stifled by Doug's cock. Her body trembled, her orgasm at its peak. But Paula did not pull away. Instead, with her mouth still locked to Catherine's sex, and her fingers still in her vagina, she scrambled around so her legs were alongside Catherine's head. Doug understood what she wanted to do and without a word, pulled his cock out of Catherine's mouth and moved away, allowing Paula to swing her thigh over Catherine's shoulders and supplant his sex with her own, squirming her labia down on Catherine's mouth.

Catherine's reaction was instant. Her tongue plunged into Paula's labia. She brought her hand round to Paula's buttocks, caressed them briefly, then pushed two fingers into her vagina.

It was Paula's turn to moan. The circle was complete, the two women joined. The sensations were so strong, the pleasure so acute that Paula's body lurched towards orgasm almost the moment Catherine's tongue touched her tenderised clitoris. She could feel her friend's heavy breasts pressing against the tight material of the basque. She could feel her fingers pushing up into her vagina, not pumping up and down this time, but scissoring them apart to stretch the inner dimensions of the silky, tight tube.

Paula tried to match her own actions to Catherine's, using the same tempo with her tongue on her clit, and doing the same thing with her fingers. But it was increasingly difficult. Her excitement was mounting so rapidly, it made it hard to concentrate. She felt wild and wanton, and dissolute, so far removed from the bounds of what she had always thought of as acceptable behaviour, that she might have well been on another planet, where different rules applied. But that only added fuel to the fire of her passion. It was her choice, she had made this decision for herself. That excited her perhaps most of all. She had stepped over an invisible line drawn in the sand, and she had done it in pursuit of her pleasure, because that mattered to her now. It was no longer to be sublimated to ambition or anything else.

Her body began to shudder against Catherine's. As Catherine's tongue and fingers worked at what felt like the very core of her, her orgasm blossomed. She tried to fight it, tried to concentrate on Catherine's body and her feelings, but it was impossible. She reared her head up from Catherine's sex, arching her back to the demands of the orgasm that took hold of her, her whole body rigid, her thighs clasped tightly around Catherine's face, holding her there until the sensations had run their course. The circle was broken, but only temporarily. As soon as Paula was capable of doing anything again, she dropped her mouth back on to Catherine's labia, and licked the long furrow between them, forcing the whole breadth of her tongue into it.

She had only experienced this sensation once before but it was different this time. Very different. When she had taken

Catherine to her bed last week it had been before Ranji, before all the exquisite pleasure she'd had with him. She hadn't known what a man could do for her then. But now she knew. Now she was alive. The sleeping beauty had been awoken with a kiss. And now there was a new element in the equation. She was intensely aware of Doug. She could feel the presence of his body. She thought she could feel the heat radiating from his cock. She knew he was watching them intently. His eyes seemed to burn into her. Before the experience with Catherine had been complete, a thing of beauty in itself. Now it was only a stage, one element in a complex sexual gavotte.

Doug timed his intervention perfectly. He inched up behind Paula and reached out until his hands were caressing her back, smoothing over the tight white basque then down to the flesh of her buttocks, circling it with his palms. They moved on to her thighs, and the contrasting texture of the lace welts.

'Lovely,' he muttered.

Paula felt Catherine's fingers being pulled from her vagina. She knew they had done this before, that they were practised in the art of this sensual dance, their movements co-ordinated. She had no idea what they would do to her, what physical combinations would be possible, but as Doug moved forward, as his cock dug into her buttocks, she knew immediately what was going to happen. He was going to take her like this, with Catherine's face still under her sex.

His fingers gripped her hips, just below the satin edged hem of the tight corset. His cock nestled into the crease of her labia, his knees splayed apart, his body crouching over her. Raising himself slightly he positioned his glans at the mouth of Paula's vagina, then slowly pushed forward.

Paula moaned. She was being filled again, reamed open,

every inch of her sex crammed, the piston of his cock moving inexorably forward until it could go no further.

The circle had become a triangle. Paula felt Catherine's mouth slip down from her clitoris. It fastened on to one of Doug's balls, sucking it gently, then reeling in the other until they were both in her mouth. The effect on Doug's cock was instant. It spasmed. It swelled, increasing its length and breadth, stretching the inner dimensions of Paula's sex and making her gasp. The explosion of hot air this produced fanned against Catherine's clit. Each action had a precise and equal reaction.

They became a heaving, sweating, moaning three-headed monster. As Doug began to thrust in and out of Paula's body, his own urgent need asserting itself, Paula initiated the same movement in Catherine's sex, pushing her fingers in and out while she sucked on the tiny lozenge of Catherine's clitoris. The hard sword of flesh buried inside her felt wonderful, but then so did, by contrast, the melting softness of Catherine's sex, and her prone, trembling body. Paula could feel Doug's semen pumping into his cock, at least that's what she thought it was, and knew his ejaculation was near. In her mind's eye she had a vivid picture of it plunging into her sex, her labia stretched thin to accommodate it, and Catherine's face beneath it, her eyes seeing everything, her mouth urging him on with little nibbling kisses.

The closer Doug got to his climax, the more he pounded into Paula, and the more Paula reciprocated with Catherine. It was not altruistic. For reasons she did not understand she needed to do it, getting as much stimulation from giving as receiving.

In fact, though they were all close, it was Catherine who came first. Paula felt her body stretch out under her, her muscles suddenly rigid, her clitoris pulsing and her vagina spasming, her big breasts trembling against Paula's belly.

Doug could see it and feel it. As Paula pulled her head up from Catherine's sex, straightening her back, he began to stroke into her with even more force, his cock butting into the neck of her womb on every inward thrust.

But Catherine did not take long to recover. She squirmed out from under her friend and knelt beside her. With her left hand she reached down over Doug's bottom and grasped the sac of his balls. Her right hand delved under Paula's body, pulling her right breast out of the bra and cupping it in her hand. She found the nipple and pinched it hard, sending a shock of pain through Paula's body, so sharp it made her sex clench around Doug's cock. At the same time she mashed her hand against his balls, grinding them against his crotch.

'Come for me,' she said, looking into Doug's eyes.

Paula felt his cock begin to spasm instantly. He pushed forward driving it as deep as it would go, wriggling up into her until every last inch was buried in her and she could feel his pubic bone hard against her buttocks, his hands pulling her back on to him at the same time. He did not move again. He stayed jammed in her, completely filling her, his glans twitching.

Suddenly Paula felt a strong kick, right in the depths of her. It was so strong it took her breath away. It was followed by another and another. Each was accompanied by a roar of noise from Doug, a cry of triumph mixed with what sounded almost like pain. His body was rigid, his fingers clamped to her hips like steel vices. His cock twitched again and again, each time with less force.

Paula had known his ejaculation would bring her off anew. She'd looked to her side, staring at Catherine, wanting her to see how beautifully she came. It was, after all, her initiative that had created such a perfectly attuned response where once there had been none.

'Catherine . . .' she said, her voice falling away as the exquisite feelings arced through her body, concentrated around the hard phallus impaled in her sex, shooting through her clit and up to her breasts, where Catherine's fingers still held one of her nipples. It seemed to last forever.

'Alma Klein, please.'

'One moment,' the switchboard operator at the Dorchester said politely.

'Hello,' a second voice said.

'Is Ms Klein there, please?'

'Who's calling?'

'Paula Lindsey. I believe Mr Latimer spoke to her about the fact that I would be calling.'

'Ms Klein isn't here right now.' The voice was female and American.

'Do you know when she'll be back?' Paula asked.

'I don't think she's coming back at all.'

'I thought she wasn't going back to New York until Monday?' Paula felt her heart sink. If Klein had changed her plans she might have missed her only chance of getting her job back.

'She is. But she's visiting a friend at the moment and I'm not expecting her back.'

'Do you have a number?'

'I'm not permitted to give out that information.'

'I understand that, but Mr Latimer told me she would be willing to talk to me.'

'I'm sorry.' The woman's voice sounded cold and uninterested.

'Could you at least let her know I called and give her my

number?' Paula asked desperately.

'I suppose I could do that,' the woman said, with obvious reluctance.

Paula gave her number. 'I'll be here all day,' she said.

'I can't promise she'll call you today, and she's on Concorde first thing in the morning,' the woman said.

'I'd be grateful if you could just give her the message.'

'Thank you for calling,' the woman said curtly.

Paula put down the phone, her disappointment extreme. Doug Latimer had kept his promise. He'd called her this morning with the news that he'd made the introduction to Alma Klein and she was expecting Paula's call. He obviously hadn't stressed the urgency of the situation. If the plan Paula had worked out stood any chance of being effective she had to see Klein before she got back to New York and made an official announcement of her plans for Winkworth's.

She was sitting in her kitchen wearing a white track suit. Considering the time she had finally got home and the exertions of the night before, she felt remarkably alert. Sex was obviously a rejuvenating elixir as far as she was concerned. It had been a long night and Doug, inspired, so he said, by the presence of two beautiful women, had proved to be an indefatigable lover. After their mutual endeavours, he had taken them both again, moving from one to the other several times. But as he'd decided it would be unfair to come in one and not the other, his final ejaculation had come as they'd both sucked and licked his cock, his semen jetting over their faces.

In the cold light of morning Paula had no regrets. In fact quite the reverse. She was delighted with her daring and bravery and with the responsiveness of her body. The one, somehow, seemed to go with the other.

She might have been tempted to kid herself that her new-found sexuality was a substitute for career ambitions, that having sublimated sex to her career for so long, the reverse would not apply. But it was not true. The ambition was still there. She desperately wanted Alma Klein to ring. She would never allow sex to slip off her agenda again but that didn't mean she could be like Catherine, content with pleasure and a Dionysian lifestyle alone. She could not see herself living off a man like Catherine lived off Doug. She hoped ambition and sex would become mutually complementary, but unless the phone rang soon she would not have the chance to find out.

She smiled to herself, remembering the money Ranji had dropped into her lap. He'd mistaken her for a call-girl once. If the worse came to the worse, perhaps that would end up being her next career move!

The noise of the phone startled her. Paula had to restrain herself from snatching it off the hook. She let it ring three times while she took a deep breath.

'Hello,' she said trying to sound cool and calm.

'Ms Lindsey?' The voice was female and American.

'Yes.'

'Alma Klein.'

'Ms Klein. It's nice of you to ring back.'

'What is it, Ms Lindsey?' Alma Klein clearly liked to get straight to the point.

'I have a proposition I'd like to put to you.'

'Concerning?'

'Your interest in thermal insulation engineering and static chip technology.'

'I must warn you that any information you have which is market sensitive could land you in a lot of trouble if used improperly.' Alma Klein's voice was as cold as steel.

'I know you are interested in Winkworth's,' Paula said.

'I think we should end this conversation now. Speculation on what my interests are and are not would not only be counter-productive but actionable.'

Paula had expected that. Alma Klein was not going to confirm her interest in Winkworth's to a perfect stranger ahead of an announcement. That could only drive the share price up through the roof.

'I appreciate that. However, I would still like to see you.'

'What is your relationship to Doug Latimer?' Alma snapped.

'We're friends, as I'm sure he told you.'

'He did.'

There was a silence on the line.

'Look Ms Klein, I am not interested in making a quick profit on the back of some deal you may or may not be doing. I have a serious proposal for you in relation to the overall structure of your business. It would take me no more than five minutes to explain it to you. I have all the relevant paperwork. If you're not interested then all you will have lost is five minutes of your time.'

Another silence, much longer this time. Paula decided not to make the mistake of filling it. She bit her lower lip and prayed.

'Have you got a pen?' Alma said.

'Yes.'

'Sixty-one Hanover Gardens. The penthouse flat. Two o'clock. Is that clear? Five minutes at two o'clock.'

The buzz of the dialling tone stung Paula's ear.

## Chapter Seven

A new dress; black with white piping along the seams, pockets and hem. New lingerie; a cream satin and lace teddy. New shoes; black suede with a spiky heel and a small silver motif in the shape of a crescent on the toe. New tights, very sheer, a subtle shade of grey with a glassy finish. New make-up, heavier mascara and eye-shadow and a touch of blusher on the cheeks. New woman, the clothes giving Paula a sense of herself she had never felt before.

As she locked her front door and got into her car Paula felt a stinging soreness as the gusset of the teddy creased into the folds of her labia. Her nipples and clitoris and labia had been sore for a week. But it was a feeling Paula relished. The soreness was a scar of a battle she had fought and won. It was a battle with herself, for her spirit, and she was proud of the courage she had displayed, and the way she had grasped, with both hands, the opportunity that had been presented to her. There was no turning back now. She couldn't say she had got what she always wanted because, until recently, she had never thought of sexual satisfaction as a goal at all, but she had certainly achieved satisfaction and revelled in the fact.

With it had come two distinct side-effects. It had undoubtedly made her more assertive and more confident. It had also bestowed her with a certain sense of relaxation, a certain detachment. The five minutes she was due to spend with Alma Klein would determine her future over the next few years but, whereas before she would have been almost totally stressed out at the prospect, now she could view it with dispassion. It was not the end of the world. There were other things in life. That didn't mean she didn't want to succeed and pull off a coup. It didn't mean she wasn't still ambitious. But things were better placed now. In the end, the shadow of Doug's phallus in her sex and the brush strokes of Catherine's tongue against her clit, still lingered on as a constant reminder not to let things get out of proportion. Her life, it seemed, was suddenly illuminated with a sense of well-being.

The street outside 61, Hanover Gardens was empty of cars, most of the residents were at their weekend country retreats, and Paula was able to park almost directly outside. The building was a Victorian mansion block with a polished brass name plate and an entryphone by the wood-panelled front door. There were at least forty flat numbers with a bell push alongside each. Paula pushed the one next to PENTHOUSE.

'Yes?'

'Paula Lindsey.'

The lock on the front door buzzed immediately and Paula pushed it open. Beyond was a small foyer and two lifts, one of which was already on the ground floor, according to the LED display over the doors. Paula pressed the call button and the metal door opened noiselessly. She rode up to the top floor.

There was only one door in the corridor outside the lift. Paula pressed the bell on the left of the door jamb and heard a clanging, old-fashioned bell ring inside. She noticed a small security camera mounted on the ceiling to one side of the door.

The door opened.

'Hello.' The girl was about eighteen, with badly cut, badly dyed, tousled blonde hair and a deep, almost orange tan that looked as though it had been acquired artificially. She was wearing an ankle-length, full-sleeved shift that was made out of a material resembling white muslin, and nothing else. No shoes. No underwear. It was easy to see that she wore nothing under the dress as it was quite transparent. Her breasts were small and almost non-existent, no more than inverted saucers but her nipples were big and knob-like. She had ragged, thick, very curly pubic hair, its dark brown colour proof, if proof were needed, that she was not a natural blonde. Her body was thin rather than slender, and her face had the haggard look of someone who had too little sleep.

'Paula Lindsey,' Paula said, a little taken back by the girl's appearance. She was definitely not what she'd been expecting.

'Ya, she's waiting for you,' the girl said. She was English with a South London burr to her voice. 'Come in.'

She stood aside to let Paula in, then closed the door behind them. The corridor was carpeted in an old green Axminster that was showing signs of wear, as did the rest of the decor, the William Morris style wallpaper peeling around the door frames, the paintwork dull and scuffed.

'She's in here,' the girl said, leading the way down the corridor, and through a door on the right.

Paula found herself in a vast sitting and dining room. There was a large Victorian dining table at one end of the room surrounded by ten or twelve spoon-backed chairs, and, at the other, a three piece suite from the fifties, upholstered in grey Dralon. The sofa was at least a five seater and was scattered with small cushions all covered in different, mostly patterned, material. Alma Klein was sitting in one corner of it.

'Ms Lindsey,' she said, emphasising the 'Ms'. 'Please sit down.' She indicated one of the armchairs to her left. She did not offer to shake hands.

Paula sat down. She had brought her papers in a small, leather document case, which she held across her knees.

'Would you like something to drink?' the girl said.

'No, Tracey,' Alma snapped. 'Ms Lindsey doesn't have time to waste.'

'OK.' The girl looked suitably rebuked.

'Well?' Alma said again displaying her desire to get straight to the point.

Paula had seen photographs of the woman in the financial press, but they did not do her justice. She was tall and statuesque with flaming red hair pinned into a severe French pleat. Her face was long and sharp, with a very straight, slender nose, slightly flared nostrils and a small mouth, the lower lip almost totally straight. She had the longest eyelashes Paula had ever seen and under them her very light green eyes seemed to burn with a life so intense it was impossible not to be drawn to her. She was dressed in a pale pink suit with a tight skirt and a waisted jacket, over a white silk blouse. Her body was lithe and slim and her legs long. She was wearing flesh coloured tights that were so sheer at first Paula thought her legs were bare.

Quite without warning Paula felt a flash of desire, a mental image of the woman lying wanton and naked, popping, unbidden, into her head. She pushed it aside hurriedly and unzipped the document case.

'Five minutes,' Alma warned, her hard stare reinforcing the point.

'It is my understanding,' Paula began, 'that you are

interested in acquiring Winkworth Holdings. It is only a good fit with your existing business if considerable and expensive changes are made to its primary manufacturing facilities.'

Paula had expected an interruption at this point. None came. Alma was looking at her critically, the lightness of her green eyes giving an impression of coldness.

'Your main interest is in the work they have been doing in insulation engineering because you have at least twenty-nine percent of the American market. Winkworth's, on the other hand, though their research and development programme has developed a new thermal insulation material, has no production facility in that area. You are interested in acquiring the company largely to get your hands on their patents. As I understand it, their thermal isolation sheeting is at least forty percent more efficient than the nearest rival – which, of course, Klein Industries produces. It is also nearly sixty percent lighter, making it ideal for automotive applications which Klein is ideally placed to exploit since you already supply Detroit with over fifty percent of their out-sourced parts.'

'So far you are merely stating the obvious,' Alma said looking at the gold Rolex on her wrist.

'The problem you would have is in starting to manufacture the product. It could be two years before you achieve the sort of volume that would bring you a return on the cost of acquiring Winkworth's. Meantime, you have paid over the odds for the rest of their business, a static chip production facility that has no synergy with your core products.'

'So?' Alma raised a carefully plucked eyebrow. She uncrossed her legs, then crossed them again with a rasp of nylon, her fingers drumming on the arm of the sofa, their nails long, beautifully manicured and varnished a light pink.

'I have a client who is looking to increase his static chip

production. He needs greater capacity. He has so many orders he simply cannot expand organically, the factory build route would take too long. He needs acquisition. He was looking at Winkworth's.'

'Too bad,' Alma said, her voice unfriendly. She looked over at the young girl who had curled herself into a ball at the other end of the long sofa.

'My client,' Paula continued undaunted, 'owns Fahrenheit Fabrication.'

'Look, Ms Lindsey, I am really not interested in hearing a list of your client's assets.'

Paula was surprised Alma Klein hadn't heard of Fahrenheit. She'd expected her to react to the name. 'You haven't heard of Fahrenheit?'

'Should I?'

'I would have thought your research people would have pointed it out to you as the biggest manufacturer of Lynol in Europe.'

'Lynol?' The expression on Alma's face changed.

'Yes.'

'Where is their factory?'

'Stockholm.' She saw the excitement go out of Alma's face. But she was about to restore it. 'And they have just opened in Toronto.'

'All right,' Alma said. She smiled a thin, weak smile. 'Now you have my attention.'

Lynol was the biggest component in Winkworth's new thermal insulator. Paula had read the patent. The manufacturing process for it could be directly adapted from the Lynol production line. Using Fahrenheit's factories, mass production could be achieved in weeks.

'My client might be prepared to sell you Fahrenheit in exchange for two things.'

'Which are?'

'Your stock in Winkworth's and a deal with AutoTech Marketing to distribute static chips in the US.'

Paula had finished her pitch. She looked from Alma Klein to the little urchin creature at the other end of the sofa. Her knees were pressing against her breasts and Paula could see the line of her buttocks under the white muslin, and tufts of pubic hair between her legs. There could be a hundred factors that she had no way of knowing about, which would make her scheme unworkable. She waited for Alma Klein to raise objections.

'I think you deserve a drink,' Alma said quietly. She got to her feet and smoothed down her tight skirt. 'Champagne?'

'Thank you.'

The floor of the large room was covered with old, badly battered parquet and the occasional worn, faded rug. Alma's cream high heels clacked on the wood as she disappeared into the kitchen.

'She likes you,' Tracey said. 'I can tell. She gets a look in her eye. She's really hot for you.'

'I'm sorry?' Paula said.

'You'll see.' She bounded up from the sofa and headed for the kitchen. A moment later Alma appeared with three different-shaped wine glasses. Tracey followed her out with a bottle of *Veuve Clicquot* champagne in her hand.

'Why don't you get some proper glasses?' Alma said testily. 'I told you to buy whatever you wanted.'

'Does it matter?'

'You should get this place done up.'

'Don't start on all that. I like it like this.'

'I don't,' Alma said. She put the glasses on the coffee table in front of the sofa and sat down.

Tracey sat beside her, twisting the wire off the cork. She

opened the bottle with surprising dexterity and poured the sparkling wine without spilling a drop. 'Used to be a waitress,' she said looking at Paula. She handed the largest of the glasses to her.

Alma picked up a glass and raised it. 'Fahrenheit's a new one on me. It's interesting,' she said. 'I pay guys thousands of dollars to research this stuff.' She looked at her watch. 'I've got to make a few calls. Are you under any time pressure?'

'No,' Paula said.

'Good.' Alma took her glass and walked out into the hall.

'She's got a sort of office,' Tracey explained. 'Fax, phones, computer. Had them all installed when she bought me this place.'

'She bought this for you?' Paula tried to sound uninterested.

'Yeah. She keeps pestering me to get it done up, like. She'll pay for anything I want. I mean not just furniture and stuff. Anything. Jewels, clothes, knickers. But I'm not that interested. Never really been into things.'

'Where did you meet?' It was pretty obvious that Tracey and Alma's relationship was far from platonic. Paula had read everything she could find on Alma Klein and her business in the last week but she hadn't come across any mention of her private life. She imagined that she hired an expensive firm of public relations consultants backed by an equally expensive lawyer to make sure that her sexual orientation remained private. She hadn't come across a single hint that she was gay in any of the articles she'd read.

'When I was waitressing. She came into this place I worked, on the make. Alma always gets what she wants. She wanted me. I was living in a bedsit. That wasn't really convenient so we got this place. She doesn't like doing it in hotels. She's scared the staff might put two and two together. Well that's what she says. The real reason is, she's ashamed of me. Doesn't want her smart friends to see me. You're the first who's ever come here.'

Paula found herself imagining the odd, waif-like girl in bed with the sophisticated and elegant American. It gave her an odd sensation, a peculiar mixture of repulsion and attraction. She couldn't work out which of the two emotions were stronger.

'I'm sure that's not true,' Paula said in an effort to sound sympathetic.

'It's all right. I don't care,' Tracey continued though it was patently obvious from the sound of her voice that she did. 'I know what she wants from me and I don't mind giving it to her. I mean it ain't as though I don't have a good time too. But she won't let me go out to work and I miss that.'

'She's not here much, is she?'

'But she calls me day and night. Really wicked stuff too. Like what she wants to do to me. Gets off on it.' Tracey giggled like a little girl. 'I shouldn't be telling you this, should I?'

'How long have you been with her?'

'Six months.' Tracey lowered her voice. 'She's great really, and really sexy.'

'I've got New York looking into a few things. They're calling me back. Has she been telling you all my secrets?' Alma strode back into the room.

'No, no,' Paula said quickly.

'I told her how good you were, Al, that's all right, isn't it?' Tracey looked very worried suddenly.

'Sure it is,' Alma said. She came over to Tracey and stroked her hair, her face softening. 'She's a good girl,' she said to Paula.

'Except when I'm bad,' Tracey said. Her hand moved up between Alma's knees, pushing her skirt up slightly.

'Tracey, you'll embarrass our guest,' Alma said, but did nothing to push her hand away.

'I'm not embarrassed,' Paula said. Another emotion surfaced. But this time it was not ambiguous. It was desire.

'Really?' Alma said, smiling. 'Most women would be. Does that mean you're gay?' Alma's eyes looked directly at Paula, with the intensity of a laser beam.

'No,' Paula said. She thought of adding a coda to that but decided against it.

'Oh,' Alma's face registered her disappointment. 'It's a pity. You're a very attractive woman. There is something about you . . .' She sat down next to Tracey.

'What, exactly?' Paula asked not wanting to let the subject drop. She felt a little like a fly taking its first tentative steps into the web of a spider.

'I think she's very sexy,' Tracey said. Her hand worked its way along the back of the sofa until she could stroke Alma's neck. She must have connected with a sensitive spot as Paula saw the American arch her head back involuntarily.

'Sometimes you meet someone who's on the edge, who is prepared to take risks . . .'

'And that's what you think about me?' Paula asked.

'Yes. Am I right?'

Paula's heart began to thump. She wasn't sure how she should answer. The truth would lead her deeper into the web.

Tracey twisted her other hand up under Alma's skirt.

'No,' Alma said, catching her wrist.

'You like it.'

The American's fingers loosened their grip but did not relinquish it entirely. Tracey stroked the inside of Alma's knee, then leant forward and kissed Alma's neck, very lightly.

'Well, Ms Lindsey? Am I right?'

Paula had no idea what she should do. Her mind told her she should politely excuse herself and leave, saying she'd wait at home for Alma's call. Her body wanted to stay. She could not pretend that she was not aroused by the two women. When she had first seen Tracey she was put off by her appearance, and found it hard to imagine what Alma saw in her, but as she watched her now, sinuously caressing the American, she thought she knew. There was a sensual quality about the girl, a raw sexuality that was extremely attractive. It was certainly attracting her.

'I think I should go,' she said weakly.

'Don't go,' Tracey said. 'You can watch. You don't have to do anything. We love to be watched.'

Alma's light green eyes looked at Paula quizzically. There was no need for Paula to ask what the question was.

'Come on,' Tracey said, taking the initiative. 'Let's go next door.' She sprung to her feet and pulled Alma up with her. Very deliberately she stretched up on tip-toe and kissed Alma on the mouth, sucking loudly on her lips, before pushing her tongue through them. As she kissed, her hands rucked up the back of Alma's tight skirt until Paula could see a pair of white panties under the tights, the cloth pulled tightly into the cleft of her buttocks.

Breaking the kiss, the two women turned and walked out of the room without giving Paula another glance. It was up to her. She could leave or she could stay. She couldn't kid herself that if she left the deal would collapse. She had clearly impressed Alma with the information about Fahrenheit Fabrication. The deal was definitely in play, Alma's American office working frantically to confirm what Paula had told her. The choice was not dependent on anything except her own desire.

Paula got to her feet. She picked up the champagne and wandered over to the window, sipping the chilled wine. There was a view over the rooftops of Mayfair, dusted with the remnants of the recent snow. Paula had sought to convince herself that her enjoyment of sex with Catherine had occurred purely because of her feelings for her oldest friend. On the basis of what had happened with Ranji and Doug, the pendulum had swung from believing she was an outright lesbian to the much more limited idea that homosexual sex was something that would only be desirable or pleasurable with Catherine.

What she had felt in the last few minutes had contradicted that idea. The sight of Tracey and Alma together had produced a strong knot of desire in the pit of her stomach. Her body hummed out a pleasant, sensual tune in a minor key. It knew what it wanted even if her mind disagreed.

The problem was admitting to herself that she was bisexual. If she walked into their bedroom, if she had sex with two strangers, she could not hide behind the excuse of her long-term friendship with Catherine. It would be an action motivated purely by homosexual desire. She remembered what Catherine had said, about needing a lot of sex, and women being nothing more than an alternative to men. It appeared that Paula's body had come to feel the same way. Now she had discovered its capabilities she was determined to exploit them to the full at every opportunity. The humming in her body, a rhythm that affected her profoundly, changed key, became sharper and more difficult to ignore.

With remarkable calmness she walked out into the corridor. Immediately opposite the door to the sitting room was another door which had been left open. Inside was a room completely out of character with the rest of the flat. It was lined with grey plastic panels and had a grey lino floor.

# THE WAYS OF A WOMAN

On a large, modern L-shaped desk was a telephone console, a fax machine and a computer. The fax machine was in the middle of spewing out a ream of paper.

All the other doors in the corridor were closed except the one at the far end which had been left ajar. Paula walked down to it. She pushed it open and went inside, finding herself in a large bedroom. Like the sitting room the furniture looked as though it had come from a secondhand sale. There was a huge Victorian wardrobe, and two enormous, mahogany chests of drawers. The bed, on the other hand, was brand new, very wide and low to the floor. It had been stripped of the top bedding and was covered with a single white sheet that looked as though it might be silk.

Alma Klein was lying stretched across it on her back. She was still wearing the skirt and blouse but her jacket, tights and white panties, and her shoes lay in an untidy heap by the foot of the bed. Tracey was naked. She knelt on the bed with her mouth pressed to Alma's sex, while Alma's legs were hoisted up over her shoulders, her ankles crossed over her back.

Feeling a little self-conscious, Paula sat on the edge of the bed. Alma turned her head to look at her.

'She's very good at this,' she said, matter-of-factly. She was undulating her hips as the young girl worked on her. 'Knows just what I like.'

'Mmm . . . love it,' Tracey murmured without looking up.

Alma reached out and touched Paula's hand. 'Are you just going to watch?' she said.

'No, I don't think so,' Paula said.

'You've done this before, haven't you?'

'Yes, but I'm not gay,' Paula said defensively. 'I just . . .' She could think of no words to explain what she felt.

'You just like sex. I know. So why don't you kiss me?'

Paula leant forward. She looked into the redhead's eyes and felt an overwhelming wave of passion. What the woman was feeling, what Tracey was making her feel, was etched into her expression, tiny crows' feet appearing at the corners where her eyes had narrowed. Slowly Paula brushed her mouth against Alma's, gradually increasing the pressure. When she dipped her tongue between her lips she was astonished by its heat and wetness. Any hesitation she might have felt was swept away. She kissed Alma harder, squirming her mouth against hers, revelling in the sensation of kissing a woman again, only the second woman she had ever done this to.

'Beautiful, beautiful,' Alma said forming the words without entirely breaking contact with Paula's mouth.

Paula stood up. She took off her new dress then stripped off the cream satin and lace teddy. She pulled down her tights. Sitting on the bed again she kicked off her new shoes and tugged the tights off her feet. She felt the same emotions as she had with Doug, astonished at her own daring, and proud of it too, glad she was prepared to act without scruples, prepared to carve out her own way of life, and not be inhibited by what others might think.

'You're a real surprise package,' Alma said, admiring her nakedness.

'Mmm . . . look at that,' Tracey said raising her head. 'I wish I had tits like that,' she added before resuming her ministrations.

'She's right, lovely tits,' Alma said her hand cupping one of them. Her touch made Paula shudder. 'Very firm. I like that. Come up here honey, let me get at you.' Alma stuck her tongue out and wiggled it up and down obscenely, the facade of sophistication giving way to something more basic.

Paula knelt on the bed. She scrambled over to where Alma lay and opened her knees, crouching directing above the American's face. With her pulse racing she lowered her sex down on to her mouth. Immediately she felt Alma's tongue delving into her labia. It found her clitoris and pressed it back against the pubic bone, her tongue unbelievably hot.

Paula felt her body lurch into a new dimension of feeling. Alma's tongue didn't stroke her clitoris like Catherine's had done, but seemed to be intent on drilling into it, the tip wriggling from side to side.

Tracey pulled herself up, lifting Alma's legs from her shoulders one by one then kneeling at the side of her body. Paula saw that her hand had replaced her mouth on the American's sex, her finger buried deep in what were rather thin labia. She could see it moving up and down, stroking against her clitoris with absolute regularity. Her other hand reached forward and grasped Paula's left breast.

'Do you come quickly?' Tracey said.

'Yes.' Paula was coming already. It was impossible not to. Alma's tongue was boring into the most sensitive spot in her body. Great waves of sensation flooded over her. But it was the newness of all this, the fact that she was allowing these two women to touch and caress her so intimately, that was the most exciting thing of all.

'You like this?' Tracey asked. Her fingernails pinched at Paula's nipples, moving from one to the other. The flash of pain turned to tingling pleasure. It arced down to her clitoris. Her body shivered. The tremors did not die away but deepened, her orgasm taking control, every nerve singing with pleasure, the suddenness of it all increasing the paroxysms that shook through her. Then she felt herself melting, her sex seeming to mould itself to Alma's mouth, her juices running out of her body and over the American's face.

It had all happened so quickly. One minute they had been sitting sedately discussing business, the next they were locked in a naked embrace.

Paula collapsed on to the bed, lying on her back. She looked at Tracey and saw a knowing, artful expression on her face. In the outside world Tracey might be young and unworldly, but here, in bed, there was nothing she did not know. As Alma sat up, the girl began to unbutton her blouse, and peel it from her shoulders. The American wasn't wearing a bra. Her breasts were small but she had large dark areolae around each stiff nipple. Tracey's fingernails pinched each of them, as she had done a few minutes before with Paula, her long, dark-red varnished nails, sinking into the tender flesh.

'I'd like to see you two together,' Alma said looking directly at Tracey.

'Mmm . . . great,' Tracey said. She scrambled over to Paula, her tiny breasts quivering. 'Tell me what you like,' she said. She brought her hand up to Paula's cheek and kissed her on the mouth. Paula tasted the sweet, musky flavour of Alma's sex.

'This is all very new to me,' Paula said. It was certainly too new for her to have established preferences.

Alma stood up. She knew what she wanted to see and she was used to getting her own way. She opened the top drawer of a rickety bedside chest of drawers and extracted a dildo. It was large and pink, its shaft curved, moulded to represent a penis, anatomically correct in almost every detail. There was a small slit in the top of the glans, and a distinct ridge dividing the glans from the rest of the shaft. The shaft itself had been gnarled to resemble a network of prominent veins and, at the base, which flared out into a flat, triangular shape, the rubbery plastic had been distressed to give the appearance of hair.

Alma tossed the dildo on to the bed. She pulled something else out of the drawer and dropped that on the bed too. It was a flesh coloured triangle, the size of a woman's pubis. Attached to each corner of it were black, elasticated straps. In the centre of the triangle was a large hole.

'I love this,' Tracey said. She picked up the dildo and the harness. The flared base was made to match its slightly curved profile. Tracey rolled over on to her bottom, and fitted her feet through the straps, pulling them up to her thighs, then kneeling again to tug the harness the rest of the way up her hips. It fitted like a pair of panties, the triangular base completely covering her pubis, the dildo sticking out from it as if she had suddenly grown a large cock.

Tracey took the shaft in her fist and began to caress it, forming an 'o' with her thumb and forefinger, and moving it up and down.

Paula's reaction to these developments had been one of total fascination. But the sight of the thin body of the urchin girl, with her flat breasts and boyish hips, now adorned with an artificial phallus, gave her already inflamed senses a new twist of arousal. It was as though she had come full circle. The dildo, Catherine's dildo, had started a long chain of events. The idea of having one take her like this, take her as a man would do, was thrilling.

'What do you want me to do?' she said, her voice husky with desire.

'Get on all fours,' Tracey said.

Paula obeyed. Tracey moved behind her, and Paula felt the dildo nudge into her buttocks. It felt cold. 'Does it vibrate?' she asked.

'Of course,' Alma said. 'Turn it on for her, honey.' She was standing at the foot of the bed looking down at them.

Tracey reached inside the plastic triangle, pulling it away

from her body, and flipped a small switch set under the flared base. The dildo started to vibrate, a muted humming filling the air. Paula felt it oscillating, strongly, against her buttocks. Her sex clenched in response.

'Nice, isn't it?' Tracey said. 'It's right on my clit. Makes me feel all mushy inside.'

The girl pushed the dildo down between Paula's legs, using her hand to guide it. The vibrating shaft butted against her labia. Looking down, Paula saw the glans projecting out from the apex of her thighs. She felt the vibrations seize her clit so powerfully it made her catch her breath. She remembered vividly the first time she had experienced this sensation and what it had done to her. Oddly, she thought, it had not been repeated. She made a mental note to ask Catherine were she could buy a dildo. She imagined lying on her own bed with a large vibrator jammed against her clitoris. The image made her shudder. How wonderful it was to be so open and alive to sexual arousal, to be able to feel so much. Her once numbed and befuddled sexuality seemed to be making up for lost time.

She wriggled her buttocks against Tracey, impatient to feel the dildo slide up into her vagina.

Tracey took the hint. Using her hand she positioned the head of the dildo against the open maw of Paula's vagina. There was no need for extra lubrication. Paula was wet enough. Her juices anointed the prosthetic glans, making it glisten. Bucking her hips, just like any man would do, Tracey forced the vibrating dildo inward.

The effect on Paula was extraordinary. The dildo reamed into her body in one smooth, effortless movement. She remembered thinking that no man had ever filled her the way the dildo had, the first time she had one thrust into her. That wasn't true now. Its effect had changed. Now it brought back graphic memories of how Ranji and Doug had felt, as they'd plunged into her. This was the same, and yet fundamentally different too. The vibrator reached right to the top of her vagina, butting against her cervix, its base stretching her labia apart. The vibrations acted on every part of her sex, but the very top of her vagina and her clitoris were the most sensitive and they reacted most powerfully. The feelings from both then seemed to merge, the singular greater than the sum of its two parts.

'You see,' Tracey said, beginning to pump the dildo back and forth. 'There's a little . . . spur . . . right up . . .' Her hands gripped Paula's flanks with more strength than she looked capable of. '. . . against . . . my . . . clit!'

Suddenly, the girl plunged forward again, but this time she did not pull back, instead she jammed the dildo deep into Paula's body and crushed it against her own, her fingers holding Paula so firmly she could not move. Not that she wanted to. She knew Tracey was coming. The girl's body began to shake, her belly and breasts quivering. She opened her mouth to moan with pleasure but no sound came out.

It was enough to set Paula off too. The vibrations from the dildo seemed to be enhanced by the subtle movements of Tracey's body. Paula felt the head of the phallus squirming around at the very core of her body. Her sex contracted around it. Her clitoris was no less involved. It felt as though it had swollen to new dimensions, distended and engorged. It had set up a contra-pulse, a counterpoint to the ceaseless vibrations of the phallus.

On the very edge of orgasm, Paula looked around to find Alma. She had dropped into an old, frayed armchair at the side of the bed. Her legs were hooked over its arms, obscenely, her sparsely haired sex wide open. She was holding a dildo in her vagina with her left hand, so deep only the stub end of it was visible, while her right pressed a much smaller, gold coloured one against her clitoris. Her eyes roamed the tableau in front of her, sparkling with feverish excitement.

Paula had never seen anything as blatant in her life. It was obscene. It was lewd. But it was also profoundly arousing. She was surrounded by sex, immersed in it. The vibrations in her vagina had turned her nerves into tingling needles of pleasure, so sensitive the feelings were almost unbearable. Almost but not quite. She felt a huge jolt of sensation from her clitoris that set her already tortured nerves alight. A flood of pure pleasure engulfed her, the fact that this was all so new, so *outré*, so out of character for her, giving the physical sensations an added poignancy. She felt everything at once, her nipples, her clitoris, and the tight, wet, silky tube of her sex, all reacting with raw passion, as her second orgasm swept her into a world of pulsing, crimson joy.

# *Chapter Eight*

It was a ridiculous thing to do. It was late when she left Alma and she should have gone straight home, but Paula wasn't thinking logically.

She parked outside the hotel and gave the commissionaire a twenty pound note to look after her car. He saluted and told her it wouldn't be a problem but by the time he'd said it, she was already racing in through the revolving doors.

She almost ran to the lift, trying to remember which floor it was. Two or three? Inside the lift she stabbed the button for two. There had been a reproduction Stubbs outside the lift doors on the right floor. She remembered it distinctly. If that wasn't on the second floor she'd try the third.

It was. The doors opened and she saw the painting, two chestnut horses standing side by side being attended by a groom. She remembered it was to the left but couldn't remember the room number. She supposed she shouldn't have been so impulsive. She should have gone to reception but she suspected they would have insisted on ringing the room and she didn't want that. This had to be a surprise.

She strode along the corridor. How far down had they gone? She thought the door had been red. Halfway along there was a red door, but hadn't it been nearer to the end? Paula hesitated. The room number, 210, was familiar. She would have to take a chance. She rapped on the door twice.

There was movement inside. She thought she heard a television being turned off. Then the door opened. Ranji stood in front of her in a white towelling robe. His face changed from surprise to delight. 'Paula, what are you doing here?'

'Thank God, you're in,' she said.

She walked past him into the room. He closed the door.

'What's the matter?' he said picking up on her very obvious agitation.

'Ranji, please, you've got to fuck me.' Paula threw herself at him, wrapping her arms around his neck and kissing him so hard their teeth clashed. She plunged her tongue into his mouth and tried to get it as far down his throat as she could.

He didn't need to be asked twice. Without breaking the kiss, he stooped and slid an arm under her knees, scooping her up as easily as if she were a feather pillow.

'Oh, God,' she moaned against his lips. It was her fantasy again. Being carried. Her body pulsed. Her heart was racing. Only Ranji had ever picked her up physically like this but there was something about it that took her breath away. She was already in a terrible state. This only served to increase it.

He carried her through to the bedroom and lowered her gently on to the bed. Her skirt rode up over her thighs and he stared down at her naked sex. Her tights and the lace teddy were in her document case in the car.

She sat up, caught hold of the sash of the robe and unknotted it. Pulling the robe apart she stared at his cock. That was what she needed more than she'd ever needed anything. She dipped her head and gobbled the still flaccid organ into her mouth, sucking it in, sweeping her tongue across the ridge under the glans. She could feel the blood pumping into it rapidly as it began to swell. Her hand looped around his scrotum. Without pulling away she looked up at him.

# THE WAYS OF A WOMAN

'What's got into you?' he asked.

She had no intention of telling him. The truth was that the cold, inanimate dildo had left her with a desperate craving for a hot, animated cock. She wanted to feel the real thing buried inside her. She wanted to feel the wild throbbing of ejaculation and the sticky wetness of semen. She didn't think she'd ever wanted anything so much in her life. There was no time to work out the whys and the wherefores, nor did she care. She only knew that however exciting the sex with Alma and Tracey had been it had left her with a void inside her that needed to be filled.

Ranji's cock was soon fully erect. She bobbed her head up and down on it, enjoying the feeling, her mouth substituting for her vagina, and seemingly just as sensitive. Ranji's hands started to unzip her dress.

'No,' she said, pulling away from him. 'There's no time.' She threw herself back on to the bed, pulled the skirt of the dress up over her hips and spread her legs apart. She wondered if he would be able to tell from the state of her labia what she had been doing. Would they look flushed and reddened? She didn't know or care. He'd definitely be able to see her wetness. Her sparse pubic hair would be plastered back and she was sure her labia would be glistening.

Ranji did not hesitate. Pulling the robe from his shoulders and allowing it to drop to the floor, he seemed literally to throw himself on to her. His cock made no contact with her thighs, but hit the target of her vagina directly and rammed straight up it with all his considerable strength.

'Yes,' she said triumphantly. It was exactly what she'd wanted. The feeling of having his hot rod of flesh buried inside her, filling her as completely as it had done before, kicked her body into new paroxysms of pleasure.

He had picked up his cue from her. He was not gentle or

solicitous. Instead he thrust his cock into her relentlessly, pounding her fast and furiously, using his well-exercised muscles to push it as far up as it would go. He squirmed his hand between their bodies to grope her breasts under the dress. He found her left nipple and squeezed it.

Paula's whole body was convulsing. His cock was butting into the depths of her vagina, the place the vibrating head of the dildo seemed to have sensitised. Each forward stroke produced a pulsating flood of feeling as his glans knocked against it. But then every nerve in her body was tenderised, stretched and tormented, made raw by the demands of Tracey and Alma.

He pistoned into her faster and harder. She grasped his bottom, the feeling of his muscled buttocks clenching as they drove his cock forward, adding to her excitement. She was coming. Or had she already come? The first throes of pleasure as he'd entered her were so strong, it had felt like an orgasm but she was much higher now, her nerves twisted tighter, her body on the brink of a much greater release.

She could feel Ranji's cock as though her vagina had become a hand, grasping it, touching it, fingering every vein and contour. She knew he was coming too. She could feel his cock swelling, the veins hardening, the spunk pumping up into it from his balls. Each pulse was transferred from him to her, the silky wet walls of her vagina stretched around it, teased out and tingling. She could not tell whether what she felt was the same orgasm, extended and accelerated to new limits of endurance, or something entirely new, but whatever it was it convulsed her entire body. They were locked together, coming together, the feeling of one feeding off the feeling of the other, his jerking cock spurting out a seemingly endless stream of super-heated spunk, adding yet another dimension to her pleasure. Her spasming vagina, clenching rhythmically around his cock as if trying to milk every last drop of his semen out of it, each contraction the occasion for another jolt of feeling that affected her almost as greatly as the shock of his first penetration. She found herself gasping for breath, all her oxygen used up by her passion.

He could come again. She knew that. He had proved that before. Despite everything that had happened to her she wanted more. They'd order a bottle of wine from room service and she'd let him rest. Then she'd take that wonderful cock in her mouth and coax it back to erection. She'd kneel on all fours on the bed and beg him, lewdly and obscenely, to bugger her. And this time she'd force him, with all her new-found sexual guile, to come like that, to give her the only experience she had not yet had.

Monday morning. No office to go to. No routine. No clothes to lay out on the bed ready to wear after her bath. No quick coffee as she put on her coat. No driving through the rush hour. No Radio Four News as she drove through the traffic. But Paula was not alarmed. By the end of the day she knew things would be very different, one way or another.

She enjoyed the brief respite from the daily grind. She had a leisurely bath without the necessity to watch the clock and made herself a whole pot of coffee. She defrosted a croissant from her freezer and sat reading the morning paper at her kitchen table, waiting for ten o'clock. There was no point in doing anything before then.

At precisely ten, she put the paper down and picked up the phone. She knew the number by heart.

'Robert Parker's office,' a female voice said curtly. It was a direct line, by-passing the company switchboard.

'Is he there?'

'Who's calling?'

'Paula Lindsey.'

'Hold the line, please.' There was a pause. 'Ms Lindsey, I'm afraid Mr Parker is not available at the moment.'

Paula had expected this response. 'Would you tell him I want to speak to him regarding Alma Klein.'

'Hold the line.' The woman had a slight Australian twang to her voice. 'Ms Lindsey, Mr Parker does not wish to speak to you. Thank you for calling.' The dialling tone followed this last pronouncement instantly.

Paula had not expected that. She imagined Alma Klein's name might provoke Parker's interest. It meant that George Fairbrother had not mentioned to him Paula's explanation for the rise in Winkworth's share price, no doubt blaming the entire fiasco on her.

It would have to be plan B.

She went upstairs. Taking her time, she put on her make-up and got dressed. More new clothes, a suit this time in a peachy colour with a tight white body in a stretchy lycra that made it unnecessary for her to wear a bra. New shoes too, of course. The new Paula Lindsey. That's what it felt like to her.

Her boldness and daring in sex seemed to have inspired boldness and daring in other areas of her life. Where sex had always been a problem before, a nagging worry, giving her a feeling of inadequacy, the strength of her sexual feelings now seemed to fill her with a belief that anything was possible. If she could overcome such fundamental difficulties, what couldn't she do?

She left the house at twelve and drove to the Savoy, allowing them to valet-park her car. By quarter-to-one she was sipping a glass of Chablis in the American Bar, keeping a close eye on the Art Deco clock on the wall.

Robert Parker was a man of habit. At exactly one o'clock every day he was in London he would eat lunch in the Grill Room at the Savoy. He always had the same table. He always ate the same meal, a grilled Dover sole, a green salad dressed with oil and vinegar only and three boiled potatoes. A crème caramel followed. No wine. A double expresso coffee ended the meal. Paula had been to the ritual lunch twice and seen it all for herself.

At two she judged he would have finished his main course and dessert and be ordering coffee. Picking up her document case Paula walked down the steps of the mezzanine and turned right into the Grill. Parker's table was on the left at the far end of the room, a large semi-circular banquette somewhat in the American style, the seating upholstered in red plush. Parker was not alone as Paula had hoped. His guest was George Fairbrother.

Undaunted, Paula marched up to the table.

'Good afternoon, Mr Parker,' she said. 'I wonder if you might spare me a few minutes of your time.' She did not wait for an answer and slid on to the corner of the banquette.

'What the hell do you think you're doing?' Fairbrother exploded, his round, ball-like face flushing an apoplectic red. Luckily both men were sitting right in the middle of the circular table and were trapped by it. They would need to summon a waiter to pull the table out if they were to escape.

Ignoring her former boss, Paula continued. 'You will have been told I've been fired from Lichtman Terry for the way I dealt with the Winkworth's share purchases.'

'Exactly. You cost me a great deal of money,' Parker said. He was a well-preserved sixty with a full head of hair that had gone completely white. His impeccably tailored suit was dark blue and he wore a white shirt and a blue silk tie. His eyes were an extraordinary blue, the colour of cornflowers, and seemed to have a luminescent quality. 'I'm afraid you'll have to excuse us, Ms Lindsey,' he added. 'I really don't think I have anything I want to say to you.'

'Mr Parker, I don't mean to be rude. I wouldn't have come here if I could have spoken to you on the phone this morning.'

'I think you should leave immediately,' Fairbrother spluttered. 'Don't make things worse for yourself.'

'The reason Winkworth's share price went north is that Alma Klein is interested in acquiring the company,' Paula insisted.

'If you don't leave this instant . . .' Fairbrother started to summon a waiter.

'No, George,' Parker said touching his arm. 'What did you say about Alma Klein?'

'She has taken a large stake in Winkworth's.'

'Did you know this?' Parker asked Fairbrother sharply.

'It's nonsense. There isn't a scrap of evidence to indicate—'

'There's this.' Paula produced a letter from the document case on her lap. The letterhead of Klein Industries was a simple design, the two feet of the 'K' attached to the top and bottom of the 'I' to form a triangle. 'I went to see Ms Klein yesterday. We talked over her interest in acquiring Winkworth's.'

Parker threw a dirty look at Fairbrother. It was the sort of look that could kill.

'I don't believe any of this,' Fairbrother said, now clearly floundering.

'Go on, Ms Lindsey,' Parker prompted.

'I've done a lot of homework since I heard of Klein's interest. It seemed to me that Winkworth's was a strange target for her business. I couldn't work out any synergy.'

'And?' Parker said.

'I discovered their research and development department had come up with a new patent for a very light, very efficient thermal insulation.'

Parker raised an eyebrow. Like the hair on his head it was entirely white.

'I don't see what that has to do with anything,' Fairbrother said gruffly.

'Don't you?' Parker said with surprise.

'Well, I suppose . . . it could be useful . . . if . . . I mean . . .' Fairbrother tried to waffle.

'All the details are in this letter,' Paula continued. 'Klein is not interested in static-chip manufacture. But the thermal insulation patent is a perfect fit for her business. She is prepared to sell you her stake in Winkworth's in exchange for an agreement to sell her the patent once you've acquired the company.' She handed the letter to Parker.

'Why doesn't she go to Winkworth's direct?'

'She tried, apparently. They refused to sell it to her.'

'And what price does she want for her stake?'

'Item three in the heads of agreement,' Paula said. 'The current market price.'

'Ridiculous,' Fairbrother said. 'The price has been grossly inflated by her interest.'

'Oh,' Paula said sharply, 'you do admit it was her interest that pushed the share price up then?'

'The price *is* inflated,' Parker said, his eyes scanning the letter.

'As you will see, that is only part of the deal. Klein wants to buy Fahrenheit Fabrication to process the insulation material. Point Six. More important for LCC she will agree to use AutoTech Marketing to distribute static chips in the US. Point Eight.'

Parker pulled a pair of horn-rimmed bifocals from his top pocket and began reading the letter more carefully. It was three pages long. They had worked on it last night, with Klein on a conference call with her lawyers in New York. There were still details to work out but the basic framework of the deal was done.

Parker read the letter twice, slowly, mulling over each heading. Fairbrother, meanwhile, made every attempt to pretend Paula did not exist.

'May I get you something, madam?' One of the waiters had spotted Paula sitting at the table.

She hesitated.

'Please,' Parker said, looking up. 'Be my guest.'

'I'd love a black coffee.'

'Certainly, madam.'

The waiter disappeared. It was not until he had returned with a shining silver pot of coffee and Paula had finished most of her first cup, that Parker took off his glasses, put them back in his pocket and turned to look at her again.

'Young lady,' he said pompously, the tone of his voice making Paula momentarily fear the worst, 'this is brilliant work. Brilliant. I'm going to get my people on to it right away.'

Paula smiled with relief. It had worked. 'I've managed to persuade Ms Klein to stay over for a couple of days. She's flown in her New York lawyer on spec. If it were convenient she suggests you meet at six this afternoon. She's waiting for my call.'

'Perfect. Call her now. I'll be there.'

Paula took her mobile phone from her document case and dialled the number Alma had given her. It was answered by her secretary who immediately confirmed the appointment.

'Why didn't you tell me of Ms Lindsey's suspicions in

relation to Alma Klein?' Parker asked Fairbrother, his tone icy.

'Because she was unable to offer the slightest reason for me to believe it. I can't pass on every ridiculous rumour.'

'That was a miscalculation, George. A bad one.' He turned to Paula. 'Right,' Parker said. 'We've got work to do. You'd better come with me. I need to run this by my people and do some quick profit-and-loss forecasts.'

'There's just one thing,' Paula said.

'Which is?'

'As Mr Fairbrother fired me on Friday afternoon, I no longer have any official position.'

'I think we can safely assume Ms Lindsey will be reinstated with no loss of benefits,' Fairbrother said quickly.

'Could I borrow your phone, Ms Lindsey?' Parker asked.

Paula handed him the phone. Parker took out a thin black leather notebook, with gold corners. He flipped it open on the table and Paula saw it contained a single sheet of notepaper on which were neatly typed a list of names and telephone numbers. He punched one of them into the dialling pad.

'Aaron Lichtman, please,' he said into the phone. Paula saw Fairbrother's face twitch at the mention of the name. 'Aaron, Bob. Look, I think we've found a way through on the Winkworth deal. There's a problem, however. Ms Lindsey . . .' he looked at Paula, his eyes asking for her first name.

'Paula,' she said.

'Yes, Paula Lindsey . . . no, no, I know she's been fired. Fairbrother's with me now. That's the problem, Aaron. She's come up with a very imaginative approach to the whole issue. Brilliant, in fact. I have to say it would be very embarrassing for me to have to take her to a meeting with Alma Klein . . . yes, Alma Klein . . . it was her idea . . . anyway, I can hardly take her to a meeting at this level, dealing with half a billion pounds in assets, and introduce her as a . . .' he put his hand over the phone. 'What did you used to be?'

'Senior account executive,' Paula said.

'As an ex-senior account executive,' he repeated into the phone. 'I would suggest to you that you need to make her a very attractive offer in order to convince her to come back to work for you, or I will have to find another company who is willing to take her on and take this business to them. Fairbrother has contributed nothing to this whole concept except to sack its originator, and yet he is her senior. That can't be right, Aaron.' For the first time since she'd sat down at the table Parker was smiling. He was enjoying the exercise of his considerable power. There was a pause while he listened to what Lichtman was saying. He handed the phone back to Paula. 'Mr Lichtman would like to speak to you, Ms Lindsey.'

'Good afternoon, Mr Lichtman,' Paula said trying to sound cool but not feeling it. Lichtman was brief and to the point. Tomorrow morning he told her, she should come and see him first thing. She would be made senior manager in charge of acquisitions, effective immediately, and offered a junior partnership in the firm. They would discuss remuneration and fringe benefits at their meeting. He thanked her for all her good work. A little stunned by the suddenness of it all Paula punched the END button on the phone and folded it away. She had just been offered George Fairbrother's job.

'Shall we go?' Parker said. 'We've got a lot of work to do.'

'I'll cancel the rest of my appointments,' Fairbrother said.

'No, George. You stay here. There's no hurry. Have some more coffee. Pay the bill.' A waiter appeared to pull the table out and Parker got to his feet. Without a second glance at Fairbrother, he took Paula's arm. His Rolls Royce waited on the forecourt, the chauffeur holding open the back door. They sat on the back seat, side by side. 'It's going to be a long night,' he said.

It was indeed a long night. It was one o'clock in the morning by the time the heads of agreement were prepared for the lawyers to put them into a contract.

Watching Alma Klein and Robert Parker work was an education. They had not amassed their respective fortunes by luck. Their attention to detail and ability to foresee problems – even in the smallest items – and come up with solutions, was impressive. Nothing was left to chance. By two, a team of lawyers from both sides, aided by four typists, had prepared contracts ready for signature. Time was of the essence. The effect of the deal on the markets for both Klein Industries and LCC shares would be enormous and the easiest way to ensure there were no leaks was to deal with everything at one sitting.

At two fifteen the contracts were signed and a bottle of Krug champagne opened. The two principals toasted Paula Lindsey and thanked her for bringing them together so serendipitously. Parker insisted that his chauffeur should take her home, while Alma gave not the slightest hint, as they said their goodbyes, of what had taken place between them on Sunday afternoon.

'I tried you all day yesterday,' Doug said.
  'I was out,' Paula replied.
  'And this morning.'
  'Sorry. It's been hectic.'
  'How did you get on?'

Paula wasn't particularly surprised to find three messages from Doug Latimer when she finally left Aaron Lichtman's office on Tuesday morning and went back to her old office ready to pack up for her move to the top floor. She'd expected him to be interested in how she'd got on with Alma Klein.

'Much better than I expected,' she said.

'How so?'

She told him. The agreements would be made public at a press conference at one o'clock so she wasn't breaking any confidences.

'Great. That's great. So you could say you owe me a favour,' he said.

'A very big favour,' she agreed. The sound of his voice had made her pulse quicken. 'When do you want to collect?' That came out more suggestively than she'd intended.

'Tonight.'

'So soon?'

'Is that a problem?' he asked.

'What are you suggesting exactly?'

'I'll pick you up at your office at six.'

There was a tone to his voice that sounded stressed. Considering that it was his introduction that had led to her coup, she would hardly refuse him anything, but she felt uneasy about it. 'Are you bringing Catherine?' she asked pointedly.

'No. I just want to talk,' he said.

'*Talk?*'

'A drink and a talk. That's not too much to ask, is it?'

'OK, six, then?'

'Thanks.' He sounded greatly relieved.

Paula put the phone down, wondering what on earth was on his mind. She immediately punched Catherine's number into the phone to ask her but got no reply. It would be

# THE WAYS OF A WOMAN

interesting to know if he had told Catherine that he planned to see her friend. She certainly had no intention of betraying her.

Of course, betrayal was a moot point in Doug's case. She had already been to bed with Doug. In the world beyond normal social conventions, they had to invent a new morality. Presumably, given the circumstances, betrayal now meant going to bed with Doug on her own, without Catherine's knowledge, consent or presence. She wondered if that's what he had in mind and what she would do if that were the case.

Putting all her personal effects in a cardboard bank box, she called for one of the security men to take it up to her new office. When she arrived back on the top floor she discovered that George Fairbrother's name had disappeared from his office door. She was to take over his old office. Just as Fairbrother had fired her without a second thought, he in turn had obviously been dismissed just as casually. The city was a place where money talked and mistakes were not tolerated.

She was delighted to discover that she had inherited his secretary, Jean, too and did not bother to say goodbye to Julie.

After settling in, and with the signwriter painting her name on the door, she took a taxi over to the headquarters of LCC for the press launch. The boardroom had been prepared and a catering company brought in to serve the hastily summoned financial press – who were used to such hurriedly arranged announcements – with food and liquor in large quantities while both Robert Parker and Alma Klein made short speeches praising each other's foresight in reaching such mutually beneficial arrangements. Smartly outfitted waiters and waitresses circulated with trays of food and drink while Parker and Klein were pursued to elaborate on their statements by journalists anxious to establish an individual angle.

'Paula.' Paula had been talking to Gregory Harmsworth about the difficulty of growing roses – a subject she knew nothing about – when Alma Klein came up behind her and put her hand on her shoulder. 'May I have a word?'

'Of course.'

'Will you excuse us, Mr Harmsworth?' Alma said politely, leading Paula across the room. 'Bob's lent me this office,' she said as she opened a panelled door.

The office beyond was large, but unused. It smelt of newly laid carpet. There was a desk, phone and a swivel chair and two pastel colour prints. Alma was wearing a tight silk dress in a forest green with high-heeled shoes in the exact same colour. A large gold brooch was pinned above her left breast. She closed the door and leant against it.

'I didn't have a chance to thank you yesterday,' she said.

'I didn't expect it.'

'Nevertheless, you did good work. I want you to know that if you ever consider coming to work in New York there'll always be a place for you in my company.'

'That's very nice of you.'

'So that's the bullshit, right?'

'What do you mean?'

'I think you're fucking gorgeous. I've got to go back tonight. I wanted something to remember you by.'

'Like what?'

'Like this.' Alma took two steps forward, wrapped her arms around Paula's back and kissed her hard on the mouth, pushing her tongue between her lips. She dropped one hand to caress Paula's buttocks through the skirt of her grey suit. 'Jesus, you make me so hot,' she said.

'This is all very new to me,' Paula said looking into her

eyes. The kiss had excited her but she was even more aroused by the way Alma was looking at her, those light green eyes burning into her as if trying to see her soul.

'I know. I just want to leave with the feel of you, the smell of you. I want to take that back with me.' She kissed Paula again, this time just grazing her lips against Paula's mouth. 'Will you let me touch you?' she said, her voice breathy with excitement.

'Touch me?'

'Take your taste home with me?'

'If that's what you want.'

'I want much more, but that's all I can have.' Alma turned the little brass knob on the door that operated the deadlock. 'Take your skirt off,' she said in the same excited tone.

'Is this the right place?' Paula said, not at all sure what she felt about Alma's proposition.

'No. No it's not. But I need it. And I'm used to getting my own way.' The look in her eyes conveyed the sort of focused energy which would be impossible to oppose. It was no wonder she made such a formidable businesswoman.

Paula actually had no idea what she intended to do, but was not fazed. She undid the short zip of her skirt and stepped out of it. She was wearing tights but no panties. Alma stared at her legs. 'As good as I remember,' she said smiling. 'You look worried. Don't be.'

'I'm not sure what you want.'

'I thought I'd explained . . .' Alma walked up behind Paula. Very delicately she kissed her neck, one hand smoothing over the curves of Paula's bosom while the other snaked down to her waist. She delved under her blouse, found the waistband of the tights and slid her hand under it. 'You smell wonderful,' she said breathing in deeply. 'What is that perfume?'

'Chanel 15.'

'Mmm . . .' Her fingers toyed with the short hairs of Paula's pubis. She was pressing her small breasts against Paula's shoulder blades while her lips sucked and nibbled at her neck. 'Come back with me,' she whispered into her ear.

'I can't . . .'

'You will come though, won't you?'

'Perhaps.'

A single finger pushed down into Paula's labia, nudging against her clitoris. Paula felt a surge of pleasure. The finger moved on. It found the mouth of Paula's vagina and pushed into it. The suddenness and unexpectedness of all this had left Paula dry, and Alma's finger could not get very far. But it persisted, wriggling inward until Paula felt her body respond and a trickle of juices soon turned to a flood. Immediately Alma's finger thrust forward until it could go no higher, her knuckles pressing against Paula's labia.

'That's what I wanted,' she said huskily, the words breathed into Paula's ear.

For a moment her body seemed to shudder, her other hand crushed against Paula's chest, her muscles rigid, her breath exhaled loudly. Though Paula could not imagine such a thing was possible, in such a short time with such little provocation, it was almost as though she had come. Then her body softened and very slowly she withdrew her finger, and peeled herself away from Paula's back.

'Thank you,' she said.

'I don't know what I did,' Paula said because she couldn't think of anything else to say.

'It's like a test,' Alma said.

'For me?' She picked her skirt up from the desk and stepped back into it.

'No, for me,' Alma said offering no further explanation.

She looked at her watch. 'I've got to go.' She kissed Paula on the cheek, as if they were two old friends who'd casually met on the street, unlocked the door, and strode out into the board room. She ignored the journalists who still were standing in clusters together now, and said a hurried goodbye to Robert Parker. As she reached the outer door she turned back to look for Paula. She caught her eye and touched a single finger – the finger that had been buried in Paula's sex seconds before – to blow her a parting kiss.

# Chapter Nine

The shadow of her encounter with Alma Klein lingered in Paula's mind all afternoon. It lingered in her body too. Alma's finger had left an impression in her sex like a key pressed into soap. She could still feel the way her arm had crushed her breasts. It took her time to work out how she felt about the experience. It had been exciting, the fire of Alma's desire for her only too obvious, but it was frustrating too because Alma had been in too much of a hurry to finish what she had begun.

Back in her new office on the top floor, with a clear vista over the city, Paula fielded a few calls from journalists wanting her interpretation of how the new deal between Klein and Parker would affect both companies and began work on the implementation of the plan. She had tried Catherine's number a dozen times and got no reply. At six her new secretary buzzed through on the intercom to tell her that Doug Latimer had arrived and was waiting for her downstairs in the lobby.

Five minutes later, as she settled in the cream leather upholstery of the back seat of his Rolls, Paula smiled to herself. It was the second Rolls Royce in the last two days that she'd been chauffeured around in. She was getting used to the thick wool rugs, the smell of leather and the silent ride.

Doug had greeted her warmly, telling her she looked beautiful and kissing her on both cheeks, but he looked uneasy, his usual breezy confidence dented for some reason.

'It's a bit difficult,' he said settling down beside Paula as the chauffeur nosed the car out into the stream of traffic. He checked that the glass partition between the front of the car and the back was firmly closed. 'You did say you owe me a favour.'

'Yes,' she said hesitantly.

For the first time he looked directly into her eyes. She saw he was just about to say something then changed his mind.

'Say it, Doug, I'm a big girl.'

'Let's have a drink first.'

'Dutch courage. No. I want to hear what you have to say.' Paula was becoming remarkably assertive.

'It's about Catherine.'

'What about her?'

'Nothing. I mean, it's not her fault. It's just . . .'

'Just what?'

'I'm sorry, I know this is all a bit sudden. I know you're Catherine's friend. I know all that, it's just that I haven't been able to stop thinking about you, Paula. Every bloody hour, every bloody minute. Ever since Saturday. If I'd known where you lived I'd have come to see you. There's just something about you, something I can't get over.'

'What about Catherine? Have you talked to her?'

'I wanted to see you first. You see, the thing is, Paula, this is all new to me. I haven't felt like this about anyone before.'

'Isn't this a bit sudden?' Paula wasn't at all sure what her reaction to this was.

'Yes. But it's how I feel.'

The Rolls pulled up outside a flat-fronted terrace house in a small narrow back street of Mayfair.

'I thought we were going for a drink,' Paula said.

'This is my town house. Would you prefer we went to a bar?'

'No, I suppose not.' Paula wasn't at all sure that was true.

The chauffeur opened the nearside passenger door and they got out. Doug unlocked the glossy black front door and stood aside for Paula to go in first. The house was tall and narrow, and beautifully decorated, the walls in pale shades of cream and white to show off the paintings that were all individually lit with special lamps. There was a small Pissarro in the hall and a Cezanne over the Adam fireplace in the sitting room, and a large Hockney oil in the adjoining dining room. It was no wonder the house was amply protected with iron grilles over the windows, a security video camera and an alarm system that Doug was in the process of deactivating.

'This is beautiful,' Paula said finding it hard to take in all the valuables that littered the room. There was a display case in one corner filled with Georgian silver. She spotted four pencil drawings by Gustav Klimt on the back wall.

'I've always liked collecting beautiful things. What would you like to drink?'

'Red wine.'

'Not champagne?'

Paula shook her head. She had had champagne at the press conference and wanted something more down to earth. She watched as he walked through into the dining room, attached to the side of which was a large modern kitchen, the ranks of cupboards faced in bright red.

'I gave Mrs Heron the night off,' he said. 'She's my housekeeper.'

'So you've been planning this, have you?'

He came back with two large glasses and an opened bottle of Burgundy. 'I wanted to see you alone.'

'Doug, this is all very flattering, but you hardly know me.'

'Is that important?'

Paula sat on a black leather Chesterfield by the fireplace. He poured the wine, and sat down beside her, handing her a glass.

'Catherine and I have an arrangement, she probably told you that,' he said.

'Yes.'

'It's not love or anything like that. I'm a man who needs a lot of sex. I'm also very busy. I don't have time to play games with women, to court them and woo them. The arrangement worked very well.'

'But?'

'I haven't been able to think about Catherine since I met you.'

'And what does that mean, Doug, what are you suggesting?' Paula knew perfectly well, but wanted to give herself time to think. It was quite obvious from his tone earlier in the day his need to see her so urgently was more than curiosity at how the deal with Alma Klein had gone. Doug was an attractive man. He was rich and self-assured and the sort of man who was used to getting his own way. She couldn't help but be flattered by his sudden interest in her. More than that she felt a now familiar quickening of her pulse, her body reminding her that it had a new agenda. Today had been a victory for her. Wasn't it an age-old tradition that the victor took the spoils, wasn't success, after all, the most effective aphrodisiac of them all? She had triumphed over considerable adversity. Tonight, she had planned to surprise

Ranji again. Instead, it appeared Doug had planned to surprise her.

'I don't know,' he said coyly. 'I just needed to explain how I felt.'

'And how *do* you feel, exactly?'

'Just seeing you makes me breathless. I've had a hard-on since you got into the car. I don't know what you've done to me, Paula.'

'What about all the other girls you've shared with Catherine?'

'What about them?'

'Have you conceived a passion for any of them?'

'Never. Look, that was just sex. I told you, I need a lot of sex. It was exciting. I'm not denying that. But with you it was something else.'

'Just me?'

'Just you.'

Paula smiled. It was quite extraordinary. For years she had worked away conscientiously at her career, paying little or no attention to men and even less to sex. She had kept herself trim and well-exercised for health reasons, not to pander to men's ideas of what was attractive, and she had made little effort with her appearance apart from keeping clean and tidy.

All that had changed since she'd met Catherine in the car park of the local supermarket. The change had been fundamental. Not only was she now prepared to listen to her own body's demands, not too subtle demands either, but the concessions she had made to fashion had given her ample means to satisfy them.

What surprised her most was that the sexual confidence she now seemed to be broadcast, like a radio beacon, to men. The new, dark red suit she wore was tight and waisted. The jacket was buttoned and worn without a blouse, revealing a little more cleavage than she would once have dreamt of showing. The skirt was shorter too, showing a little more of her long slender thighs than would have been the case before. But though this change was measured in fractions of an inch, the real change was a matter of miles. Whereas before she had never imagined using her attractiveness as a means to any end, now she was prepared to flaunt it outrageously to get whatever she wanted. The inner confidence she had gained from the knowledge that she was as sexually capable as anyone else, was part of this process. It had become part of her body language, part of what she was, an essential constituent in the whole package. And the whole package, the whole beautifully wrapped package, she had come to realise, had given her something else she had never had before: power over men.

She looked at Doug Latimer. He controlled companies with a net worth of well over a billion pounds but if she had snapped her fingers and told him to get on his knees and lick her shoes she knew he would do it without hesitation. He would do anything for her if it would mean, as the Victorians had said, he could have his wicked way with her.

But none of that solved her major dilemma. Catherine. Going to bed with Doug was a betrayal of her friend despite the fact she had already gone to bed with him *à trois*. She couldn't kid herself that it wasn't. Paula knew what she should do. She should walk out. Catherine must be home by now. She should phone her and tell her everything that had happened. That's what she should do. Instead she sipped her wine and turned to look directly into Doug's eyes. What she saw there was a lust so strong it was like a physical assault. It was unavoidable, irresistible. To be wanted so desperately was exhilarating. Her pulse quickened for a second time.

'Where's the bedroom?' she said quite casually.

'I'll show you,' he said, about to jump to his feet.

Paula stopped him by putting a hand on his knee. 'No. Give me ten minutes. Let me get ready,' she said firmly. She put her hand on his cheek and kissed him lightly on the mouth, but pulled away when he tried to force his tongue between her lips. 'Be patient,' she said.

'I want you.'

He hadn't lied about being erect. She could see a large bulge pushing out against his flies.

'The feeling's entirely mutual,' Paula said,

'Top of the stairs, second door on the left,' he said. 'If you want . . .' he hesitated, '. . . I mean if there's anything you need, there's a lot of stuff in the black lacquered chest.' He had an impish look in his eye.

'What sort of stuff?'

'You'll see.'

'Ten minutes,' she reminded him getting to her feet. She poured herself another glass of wine then climbed the stairs. As she opened the bedroom door she felt the same sort of thrill she had felt with Alma and later with Ranji. It came from being in charge, of taking control of her own destiny.

The bedroom was decorated in matching tones of blue and green with a chequered counterpane and thick dark blue and green striped curtains, already drawn over the windows. Paula turned on one of the brass bedside lamps then closed the door. Standing against one wall was a large, modern, black lacquered chest of drawers, its corners and edges lined with brass. It had three deep, long drawers and two half drawers at the top. Each had an inset brass handle above which was a keyhole. On the top surface was a small white bowl and a large, beautifully crafted wooden box made from a dark, highly polished wood Paula could not identify. The bowl contained two brass keys.

Paula tried the top left-hand drawer. It was locked. All the drawers were locked. She inserted one of the keys into the lock of the top drawer, wondering if Doug had conveniently left the keys out as part of his preparations for this evening. She imagined the chest of drawers was locked to keep the housekeeper from opening it.

She slid the drawer open and looked inside. It contained several neatly stacked packets of stockings. They were in a variety of colours and types, hold-ups with lace welts, sheer black with seams and a fully fashioned heel, white, cream and a totally opaque black with a shiny finish. There were two or three pairs of fishnets and a couple of pairs of tights, the packet advertising that they were 'crotchless'.

Paula opened the top right-hand drawer. It contained three piles of neatly folded lingerie. There was one of panties, one of bras and one of suspender belts, all making up matching sets. They were made from satin, silk or lace and were mostly black but with a couple of sets in white and one in a bright red. The bras were large with big, voluminous cups. Paula picked the top one up and looked at the label. It was 38C, Catherine's size.

The second drawer down also contained lingerie, four or five satin and lace basques, and two piles of teddies and shimmering bodies in more exotic materials, gold lurex, sequined black satin, and a shiny metallic silver. There was also a curious garment made from sturdy white leather straps joined together by polished metal links, the shape and purpose of which, folded as it was, she could only guess at.

The third drawer down was full to the brim. It contained outer garments, though they were far from conventional. Half were made from a very fine, thin black leather, so soft it felt like fabric. There were shirts, tops and dresses. They were all low cut and/or extremely short. But as Paula rummaged through the drawer, she found even more bizarre outfits, all short, skimpy dresses in white or red. Some were backless, some designed to leave the breasts or the buttocks exposed. At first Paula wasn't sure what they were made from and picked one up. It was only when she touched the material she realised it was very stretchy, thin rubber. She suddenly remembered the shop opening Catherine had taken her to and some of the clothes available there.

The last drawer contained shoes, all, without exception, with at least six inch heels. Some were shiny black and red leather, others were red suede. There was a pair of black leather thigh boots and a crumpled pair of a similar length, made from black rubber. All, Paula noted, were Catherine's size.

The chest was a treasure trove for a fetishist, a basic kit for entertaining men. Paula had no doubt Catherine was responsible for assembling the collection. She was sure she had a bigger one at her own house. This was the economy-sized version, useful when the sudden need arose away from her home base.

Paula opened the wooden box on top of the chest. It was lined in green felt, with a built in tray that was levered upwards as the lid was opened. Neatly racked on the tray were three vibrators, in various sizes, the smallest no bigger than a finger. Under it, in the bottom of the box, was a long strip of black silk wound into a coil, a pair of metal handcuffs and two odd-looking clips with serrated jaws attached to a thin metal chain. There were also two small leather harnesses, embossed with press studs, one of which had tiny metal spikes on the inside.

The idea of getting dressed up for sex was relatively new to Paula, but she remembered vividly the effect it had had on her, how the stockings she had worn had made her sex and buttocks feel more exposed and more sensitive and how the tightness of the white basque had seemed to increase her pleasure. There was something to be said for the spontaneity of sex, for the sort of sex she had had with Ranji on Sunday night, wild and unplanned. But sex could also be ritualistic, calculated and arranged and accompanied by the appropriate vestments and totems.

She smiled to herself. Sex used to be a closed book to her; now she was beginning to appreciate its more arcane and secret mysteries.

Paula rifled through the top drawer and found what she was looking for: a pair of sheer black hold ups with black lace welts. She thought of wearing one of the *outré* rubber dresses, with her breasts hanging out and her buttocks exposed. The idea excited her but she wasn't sure whether she wanted to be that outrageous with Doug at this stage. Instead she took out a pair of black patent leather high heels. Catherine's shoe size was, fortunately, only half a size up from her own.

The en suite bathroom was tiled in tiny mosaics in a light grey. Paula closed the door and began to take off her clothes. Fingering through the clothes in the chest had aroused her as she imagined how it would feel to wear them and be seen in them. There was a large mirror behind the double wash basins and Paula's eyes stared back at her from it. She could see her excitement, playing there, like the glints of light in a diamond. There was no guilt and no regret.

Naked, she broke the seal of the cellophane packet. It made a loud crinkling sound as she drew the nylons out. She sat on the edge of the bath and rolled the sheer black nylon over her long legs, stretching it until it was perfectly smooth. The elasticated lace welt at the top was tight and dug into her flesh, creating a channel in it all the way around her thigh. She climbed into the high heels. She had never worn heels this high. They tilted her feet almost vertically, the muscles of her calves and buttocks were immediately firmed and contoured by the effort.

She looked in the mirror again. The semi-circular depressions the tight welts had made in her soft flesh left a gap directly under her sex. She could see right through it. Turning around slowly, the height of the heels forcing her to take tiny steps, she looked over her shoulder to get a view of her back. Her bottom was taut and hard, the sharp curves that jutted out from her thighs so pronounced they had formed a deep crescent shaped crease under each buttock, like two wide smiles. The shoes made her long legs look even longer. They seemed to go on forever.

The sight gave her a little *frisson* of pleasure. She tottered around again and looked at her naked breasts. Her nipples were already puckered, two knobs of corrugated flesh. She circled the palm of her right hand against each nipple in turn and felt them tingle. She slipped her left hand over her flat belly, watching in the mirror as her middle finger disappeared into the slit of her labia.

The sight of herself was arousing. That was another new element, another piece of the jigsaw that had slotted into place. She had never derived pleasure from looking at herself before, but now, especially dressed like this, dressed for sex like an expensive whore, she found it affected her deeply. Next time she masturbated, she thought, she would do it in front of the mirror. The thought made her shudder.

She heard the bedroom door open.

'Paula?' Doug's voice was tentative.

'Yes.' She opened the bathroom door and stood in the doorway, her arms akimbo. The light from the bathroom was much stronger than the light in the bedroom and she was silhouetted against it. Doug stared at her, his mouth open, his eyes roaming her body.

'You look fantastic,' he said almost in a whisper.

'Take your clothes off, Doug,' she said in a commanding voice. She switched off the bathroom light and closed the door. She was in no mood for fumbling with zips and buttons. She knew what she wanted.

Hurriedly Doug stripped off his shoes and socks. He pulled off his shirt and tie and unzipped his trousers. Paula watched as they fell to the floor. He was wearing silk briefs which were distended by the shape of his erection. Quickly he pulled them off too.

'Lie on the bed,' Paula said, in the same implacable tone. She stripped off the counterpane and duvet. The linen undersheet was pale cream.

Doug looked at her slightly askance, not knowing what to expect from her. But then he had never been to bed with her on her own. Last time she had been an enthusiastic novice, guided by Catherine. Now, it appeared, she had her own ideas and he had no way of knowing what they might be.

As Doug lay on the bed Paula walked, with tiny, diminutive steps, over to the black lacquered chest. She was aware of his eyes boring into her. She'd seen in the mirror what he could see, her tight, round buttocks and the circular gap between her thighs where the tight nylon bit into them. She wondered if he would be able to see her labia. She knew they were wet. Would he be able to see them glistening?

She opened the wooden casket and extracted the strip of black silk. She wondered how many times Catherine had stood here, bizarrely dressed in black leather or tight red rubber and selected items from the box. Were the handcuffs for him, or her? Had the ritual dressing, the donning of priestly robes for the ceremony of sex, excited her as much as it excited Paula?

She walked back to the bed. His eyes watched her breasts as they rose and fell with each step.

'What do you use this for?' Paula asked, stretching the black silk out between her hands as she knelt on the bed.

'Blindfold,' Doug said hoarsely.

The word gave Paula a shock of pleasure, the memory of how Catherine had blindfolded her so recent and so vivid. It was obviously something Catherine liked to do.

'Raise your head then,' Paula said. She wound the black silk around his head and tied it so tightly the material pressed against his eyelids. His cock twitched noticeably as he lay back on the cream linen sheet.

Paula looked down at his body, his big uncircumcised erection resting on his belly. She felt another wave of pleasure. There was something peculiarly arousing about the fact that he couldn't see her. It gave her a freedom to be even more outrageous, her actions cloaked in anonymity, impersonal and detached.

Casually, she wrapped her fist around his cock and squeezed it hard. She felt her sex contract at exactly the same time. She squeezed again, as hard as she could, and this time he moaned. She took her hand away.

'Stay where you are,' she said. The blindfold had made her remember what Catherine had done to her and she wanted to repeat the experience. She got off the bed and went back to the casket, extracting one of the dildoes from the green felt tray. It was a replica of the one Catherine had used on her.

Coming back to the bed she saw Doug's head move, trying to listen to her movements. Kneeling up on the bed again she dropped the dildo on the sheet then grasped his cock in her fist again, pulling it up until it was vertical then leaning forward and blowing her hot breath on it. It twitched. Paula pulled back the foreskin to reveal his smooth pink glans. She licked it with the tip of her tongue, then ran her tongue around the distinct ridge that separated it from the rest of the shaft. It swelled immediately.

Paula picked up the dildo in her other hand. She turned the gnarled base and it started to vibrate, its humming loud and intrusive. Experimentally she touched the dildo against Doug's cock, pressing it against his shaft. She saw his body tense. She ran the cream plastic phallus down until the tip was jiggling against his balls. Then she brought it right up to the top of his glans and jammed the point into the slit of his urethra. He moaned, his body rigid, his buttocks arching off the bed. For a moment she thought his reaction was so strong he was going to come. But that was not part of her plan so she pulled the dildo away and his body relaxed.

Paula spread her knees apart and brought the head of the dildo up to the top of her thigh, crushing it against the black lace stocking top. She felt her labia vibrate. Teasing herself, she moved the dildo over to her other thigh, again feeling the vibration transmitted through her soft flesh to her sex. Her clitoris throbbed too.

She slid the dildo into the cleft of her buttocks. She was terribly aroused. She looked down at Doug's big cock and remembered how it had ploughed into her so comprehensively. With everything that had happened to her in the last few days it was difficult to make definite comparisons, but at this moment she certainly felt more aroused than she had ever been before. It was the situation as much as the physical provocation, she knew, handling the fetishistic garments, seeing the handcuffs and strange harnesses and clips and having Doug stripped and blindfolded in front of her. It was all so new and all so thrilling. She wanted to know everything there was to know about sex, she decided. She had no idea what the clips were for or the little studded harnesses, but she was going to find out. She was going to become an expert.

Slowly she eased the dildo down between her buttocks. She felt it nudge in the dimple of her anus. It reacted with a strong stab of sensation. She was tempted to see what it would feel like to plunge the dildo deep into her rear, but resisted and moved on. Another wave of pleasure flooded over her as the oscillating plastic slipped into the mouth of her vagina. She guided it up into her sex and felt the vibrations lancing into her so strongly that she moaned, her body swaying forward. Getting herself back under control, she pulled the dildo out and slid it along the furrow of her labia until it was hard against her clit.

The vibrations engulfed the swollen bud of nerves, long tendrils of feeling streaking out from it, like the tentacles of some giant octopus, wrapping themselves around her body. She felt herself tense, the peaks and troughs of the vibration immediately matched by a more profound frequency as the first signs of orgasm coursed through her blood. God, how she loved this feeling. How could she have allowed herself to go so many years without it? But then you can't miss what you haven't had.

She allowed the waves of pleasure to wash over her, each taking her slowly, inexorably towards her climax. She stared at Doug's cock. It was twitching, responding to the tiny little noises she was making, Doug's imagination running riot.

The waves mounted higher, pulsing through her faster, the gap between them getting shorter. She was rapidly approaching the brink and she knew what she wanted now.

In one fluid movement she threw the dildo aside and swung

her leg over Doug's hip. He started at her touch. Taking his cock in her hand, she guided it up between her legs and then dropped her body down on to it, feeling it rearing up into her vagina, hard and incredibly hot. Immediately she began riding it, not caring about him, or his pleasure, mercilessly using all her strength to bounce up and down on him, her buttocks slapping loudly against his thighs, her breasts doing the same against her chest. He groaned but she didn't let up. Her orgasm didn't make her stop either. She came in an explosion of feeling, but she pounded his cock into her even more strongly, using it to intensify her orgasm. Sweat was running down between her breasts and she rode him until, finally, her body could take no more. She slowed, though it was impossible for her to stop dead, the aftershocks of orgasm needing to be soothed by a gentle descent from the heights of passion.

It was only then that she realised he had not come too. She found herself laughing. Why hadn't she found a man with real stamina like this years ago?

'Why are you laughing?' he asked.

'You're such a wonderful lover,' she told him, leaning forward and kissing him on the mouth.

She reached to pull the blindfold from his eyes, but when he felt what she was doing he caught her by the wrist to stop her.

'Not yet,' he said.

'What then?' The anonymity of the blindfold had been part of her excitement. Perhaps that's what excited him too, she thought. In the darkness behind the black silk he could imagine all sorts of things.

She pulled herself off him. His cock left her body with a loud plop. Moving to kneel at his side she took it in her hand. It was sticky with her juices. She wished she knew more about sex. Tomorrow she was going to go out and buy all the books she could find. She'd read in the newspapers about a new genre of erotic fiction. Would they be able to teach her what she was so hungry to learn?

Slowly she pulled her hand up his erection, dragging the foreskin back up over his glans, then exposing it again with a sharp downward stroke.

'Yes,' he encouraged.

She hadn't done this to a man for a long time. In the flawed sexual history of her marriage, it was the one thing she could remember that her husband had always liked. She tried to recall what she had done. As she stroked her right hand up and down the long shaft, she pushed her left hand down between his thighs, until she could grasp his scrotum.

'Oh yes,' he moaned as she squeezed his balls.

She felt his cock pulse and swell. She began to move faster, and hold him more tightly. The veins on his cock bulged. What was he imagining in his mind's eye? Was he remembering her with Catherine, their mouths pressed to each other's sexes, their bodies writhing against each other? Or was his picture more complicated, involving the handcuffs and rubber dresses and thigh-length rubber boots?

Paula didn't care. What she was doing to him was exciting her too, her body recovering rapidly from her extended orgasm, wanting more. And no reason why she couldn't have it, she thought. Without taking her hands away she shifted up the bed, positioning herself so she was kneeling above his face, her sex directly above his mouth. Without any hesitation she sank down on her haunches so that her labia were pressed against his lips.

This development produced a strong surge of feeling in Doug's cock. It jerked in her hand as she felt his tongue immediately begin to explore the crease of her sex. At first he licked the whole length of it, using the whole breadth of his tongue to spread her labia apart. Then he stuck the tip of his tongue into her vagina, squirming it up into her until he could taste her juices. But this didn't last for long. He soon centred his tongue on her clitoris. He didn't stroke it up and down but flattened his tongue against it, pressing it back against the bone and then waggling his tongue from side to side very rapidly.

Paula felt her body spasm with a new sensation. It felt a bit like the vibrator, not as sharp and strong a motion but much hotter and wetter and just as affecting. Trying to ignore the rush of pleasure it produced, Paula pumped her hand hard around his cock and squeezed his balls. She knew he was close. His cock was full of spunk. She could see it throbbing. She wanted it. She wanted to watch him come.

Suddenly she saw his glans balloon outward, as she pulled the foreskin back on a downward stroke. The slit of his urethra widened and she felt his cock kick against her fist, every vein pounding. There was a pause, everything held in abeyance for what seemed like an eternity, then a string of white spunk leapt into the air. It proscribed a parabolic arch and spattered down on his belly. A second stream was almost as powerful. She stroked her fingers up his shaft and watched more spunk leak out over her thumb and forefinger.

Doug's body relaxed, but as his own orgasm passed, he pushed his head up from the bed as powerfully as he could. His tongue pressed ever harder on Paula's clit, grinding it against her body. The sight of his ejaculation had proved a dramatic stimulus. As she felt him manoeuvring his tongue against her clitoris again, a hand slid over her buttock towards her vagina. Her senses reeled and almost before she knew what was happening, at exactly the same moment that two of his fingers thrust up into her sex, a second orgasm broke over her like a tidal wave, engulfing her entirely and knocking over everything in its path.

It took some time for her to recover. Eventually she knelt at his side and pulled the blindfold from his eyes. He blinked at the light.

'What were you thinking of?' she asked him.

'You,' he said.

'Just me?'

'You're enough for me.'

Paula didn't know whether she believed him. But it didn't matter. Even with all his sexual expertise and stamina she realised, quite suddenly, that he was not enough for her.

'Paula?'

She had been dreading the call. The sound of Catherine's voice made her go cold. She knew she should have called her but she'd been putting it off.

'Hi, Catherine, how are you?' she said, trying to sound normal.

'Listen, I need to talk to you. You couldn't come over could you? I wouldn't ask normally, but it's a bit of an emergency. I really need to talk to someone.' Catherine's voice sounded breathy and stressed.

'OK.' Paula said trying not to sound reluctant. She looked at her watch. It was seven o'clock. 'I'll be there in half an hour.'

'Great. I really appreciate it.'

'What are friends for?'

It was, Paula supposed, as she put the phone down, better to tell Catherine the truth face to face. It had been two days since her evening with Doug. She had told him, over breakfast, that though she would be happy to see him from time to time, she would not contemplate a permanent relationship with him. She was not ready for that and it might well be a long time before she was prepared to settle down. Since her sex life had blossomed so dramatically, she hadn't the slightest intention of making do with one man when she could evidently have and enjoy so many.

Despite this disappointment, Doug had insisted his relationship with Catherine was over, so Paula had made him promise to let her break the news to her friend. It was a prospect she didn't relish but she didn't want to risk Doug saying the wrong thing about her. The only way she hoped she could save their friendship was by doing all the explaining herself, though exactly what she was going to say she hadn't the faintest idea. Fortunately Doug had to go to Scotland on business for a week, so that gave her plenty of time to tell Catherine what she had to know.

Paula dashed upstairs, changed quickly from her work clothes, adjusted her make-up and brushed her hair. At seven twenty-five she parked in Catherine's drive. She took a deep breath and opened her car door. The front door was flung open as she got out of the car.

'Hi,' Catherine said. They kissed on both cheeks before Catherine closed the door against the biting cold. She led the way into the sitting room. There was a very good bottle of Italian wine on the coffee table. It was half empty. Catherine went into the kitchen to get another glass.

'Thanks for coming around,' she said.

'What's the problem?' Paula couldn't help thinking this sudden urgency was caused by something Doug had said.

'Doug.'

Damn him, Paula thought. He'd obviously blurted out something to Catherine over the phone, despite his promise not to. 'Look, Catherine . . .' She had rehearsed a little speech.

'No. It's no good. I've made up my mind.' Catherine

poured the wine, handed the glass to her friend and slumped down on the sofa beside her.

'Some things just happen sometimes . . .'

'That's the problem,' Catherine interrupted. 'You know me, Paula. Better than anyone. It's all or nothing with me, right? You know how impulsive I am.'

'How impulsive you are?' Paula didn't understand that remark.

'Yes.' Catherine paused. She looked straight at her friend. 'I've met someone else.'

'What!'

'Another man. He's gorgeous. Absolutely bloody gorgeous. I couldn't help myself.'

'You've been to bed with him?' Paula breathed a huge sigh of relief. She wasn't going to have to confess.

'Twice. He's incredible. I thought Doug was good but Franco . . .'

'Franco?'

'He's Italian. From Turino,' she said the name with an Italian accent. 'Franco Gianni. He's an importer.'

'So what are you going to do? I thought Doug paid all your bills.'

'He does. That's why I wanted to talk to you. I can't afford to live here without some help.'

'Is Franco rich?'

'Very.'

'Well, surely you can get him to replace Doug if you ask him nicely enough. That's well within your capabilities, I'd have thought. Is Franco married?'

'I don't know.'

'Didn't you ask him?'

'No. At the time I didn't care. And we haven't done a lot of talking. To tell you the truth my mouth has been full most of the time.' Catherine smiled. The smile turned into a broad grin.

'Would you mind if he was?'

'Not really. I don't think I'm in love with him but I'm definitely in lust with him.'

'Have you told Doug?'

'No.'

'Not even a hint?' Paula was beginning to wonder if Doug's sudden interest in her was caused by the fact he already knew Catherine was leaving him.

'No. He's in Scotland for a week, thank God. It gives me a chance to get things sorted out.'

'But you're going to?'

'Of course.'

'So apart from the fact that you've got to bring Franco up to speed on your financial situation, and give Doug the elbow, I don't see there's much of a problem.'

Catherine sipped her wine. Through the front window Paula saw a sleek red Ferrari pull up behind her car in the drive. 'Is this him, by any chance?' she asked.

'Yes. I wasn't expecting him. Do I look all right?' Catherine jumped to her feet and started combing her hair with her fingers. She was wearing a yellow dress with full sleeves and a knee-length skirt. She looked, Paula thought, quite wonderful. There had been a time when Paula could have admired her body objectively. That time had passed. Since she walked through the front door Paula hadn't been able to stop herself imagining the voluptuous body that nestled under that dress.

'Darling,' Catherine flung open the front door. 'Such a lovely surprise.'

'I couldn't keep away, *caro*. I couldn't stop thinking about you.'

'Come in. There's a friend I want you to meet.'

Franco walked into the room. He was tall and broad with thick straight hair, dark brown eyes, and a wide mouth with fleshy lips. As he smiled, his teeth seemed to sparkle, perhaps because of the contrast to his tanned and tawny complexion.

'Franco Gianni, this is Paula Lindsey.'

'Charming, quite charming,' he said. 'Catherine has told me all about you, of course, naturally enough, but you are everything that she had said. Most charming.'

As Paula stood up and extended her hand he took it in his and kissed it, his eyes looking up at her as he did so with more than casual interest.

'Pleased to meet you,' Paula said. She could see why Catherine had fallen for him. It wasn't that he was particularly handsome. Overall his features were a little coarse. But he radiated a sort of magnetic attraction that was indefinable but irresistible.

'Such beautiful friends,' he said turning to Catherine. 'Just looking at you makes me hot.' He slipped his arm around her waist and hugged her to him, kissing her full on the mouth.

Paula watched. She could see their tongues vying for possession of each other's mouth, both wanting to be the aggressor.

'*Caro*,' Franco said, right on cue, 'we're embarrassing your friend.' He turned to Paula and smiled. 'I am sorry for this, but passion is passion.'

It was not the way he said it but the way he was looking at her that alerted Paula. It was not a gaze of concern but of hunger. Catherine had not summoned her here to discuss her financial and emotional problems. She was quite capable of dealing with Doug and getting Franco as a substitute provider. Paula hadn't been brought round as a friend any more than Franco's arrival had been a surprise.

'She's not embarrassed, are you Paula?' Catherine said. She looked into Paula's eyes, seeing the truth had dawned on her friend. She raised an eyebrow to ask the unspoken question: was Paula going to stay?

'No,' Paula said. 'We're very old friends.'

'Is good.' Franco said.

She could have walked out the door. There was nothing to stop her. It would not mar her friendship with Catherine. It would not stop her sleeping with her on other occasions. On the other hand there was nothing to stop her from staying, from indulging the needs and desires Catherine had been responsible for awakening. In the end was there any real choice? The answer seemed to be no. There were, however, she thought, many other possibilities to the scenario Catherine and her boyfriend had cooked up. Paula caught Catherine's hand and pulled her into her arms, looking straight into Franco's dark brown eyes. 'Very old friends,' she repeated. 'Can I use your phone?'

Catherine had not expected that. 'Of course.'

Paula sat on the sofa and picked up the phone. She punched a number into the dialling pad then looked up at Catherine. She thought she could see the hardness of her nipples through the yellow dress.

'Hello . . . Room 234 please.' There was a pause. Catherine raised an eyebrow as if to ask what she was doing but Paula smiled enigmatically. 'Hello Ranji, it's Paula . . . I'm fine. Just fine. Listen, I wondered if you're doing anything this evening? No? Great. It's just that I'm here with Catherine . . . yes, Catherine, and we thought you might like to come over and join us . . . no, Doug's away in Scotland. That's great. Take down the address.' She gave him the address and hung up.

'What's going on?' Franco said.

Paula got to her feet again. She took Catherine in her arms and kissed her full on the mouth, her tongue plunging between her lips, their bodies crushed together. She could feel Catherine's small hard nipples as distinctly as she could feel her own.

'He likes to watch,' Catherine admitted.

'So do I,' Paula said firmly. 'So do I.'

*More Erotic Fiction from Headline Liaison*

# SEVEN DAYS

## Adult Fiction for Lovers

### J J Duke

*Erica's arms were spread apart and she pulled against the silk bonds – not because she wanted to escape but to savour the experience. As the silk bit into her wrists, a surge of pure pleasure shot through her, so intense that the darkness behind the blindfold turned crimson . . .*

Erica is not exactly an innocent abroad. On the other hand, she's never been in New York before. This trip could make or break her career in the fashion business. It could also free her from the inhibitions that prevent her exploring her sensual needs.

She has a week for her work commitments – and a week to take her pleasure in the world's wildest city. Now's her chance to make her most daring dreams come true. She's on a voyage of erotic discovery and she doesn't care if things get a little crazy. After all, it can only last seven days . . .

**0 7472 5094 4**

*Also available from LIAISON, the intoxicating new erotic imprint for lovers everywhere*

# Dangerous Desires

## J. J. DUKE

*In response to his command, Nadine began to undress. She was wearing her working clothes, a black skirt and a white silk blouse. As she unzipped the skirt she tried to keep her mind in neutral. She didn't do this kind of thing. As far as she could remember, she had never gone to bed with a man only hours after she'd met him ...*

There's something about painter John Sewell that Nadine Davies can't resist. Though she's bowled over by his looks and his talent, she knows he's arrogant and unfaithful. It can't be love and it's nothing like friendship. He makes her feel emotions she's never felt before.

And there's another man, too. A man like Sewell who makes her do things she'd never dreamed of – and she adores it. She's under their spell, in thrall to their dangerous desires ...

**0 7472 5093 6**

## Adult Fiction for Lovers from Headline LIAISON

| | | |
|---|---|---|
| SLEEPLESS NIGHTS | Tom Crewe & Amber Wells | £4.99 |
| THE JOURNAL | James Allen | £4.99 |
| THE PARADISE GARDEN | Aurelia Clifford | £4.99 |
| APHRODISIA | Rebecca Ambrose | £4.99 |
| DANGEROUS DESIRES | J. J. Duke | £4.99 |
| PRIVATE LESSONS | Cheryl Mildenhall | £4.99 |
| LOVE LETTERS | James Allen | £4.99 |

*All Headline Liaison books are available at your local bookshop or newsagent, or can be ordered direct from the publisher. Just tick the titles you want and fill in the form below. Prices and availability subject to change without notice.*

Headline Book Publishing, Cash Sales Department, Bookpoint, 39 Milton Park, Abingdon, OXON, OX14 4TD, UK. If you have a credit card you may order by telephone – 01235 400400.

Please enclose a cheque or postal order made payable to Bookpoint Ltd to the value of the cover price and allow the following for postage and packing: UK & BFPO: £1.00 for the first book, 50p for the second book and 30p for each additional book ordered up to a maximum charge of £3.00.
OVERSEAS & EIRE: £2.00 for the first book, £1.00 for the second book and 50p for each additional book.

Name ........................................................................................

Address ....................................................................................

....................................................................................................

....................................................................................................

If you would prefer to pay by credit card, please complete:
Please debit my Visa/Access/Diner's Card/American Express
(Delete as applicable) card no:

Signature ...................................... Expiry Date ............